STOPPING

PLACES

~ ~ ~

Stopping Places

Is written by Dr. Valerie A. Beauchene

Cover design by Robert R. Beauchene

Printed in the United States of America

TABLE OF CONTENTS

PREFACE

Ten year old Josiah was ready for another adventure with his friend Mr. Jack.

They had become close buddies the previous year as Josiah had been part of a Colorado outing with several other boys to benefit the Kurdistan people of Iraq.

Once when Mr. Jack had preached in his church he showed the pictures of these women and children and how they lived. Josiah had wept. He just couldn't hold it back. He didn't feel too badly about crying though, because, even as Mr. Jack had shared their story and pictures at the conference, he had cried too. As a matter of fact, Josiah thought that maybe there hadn't been a dry eye in the church.

But when Josiah had left the church that day and throughout the whole next day, he just couldn't get the Kurdistan people out of his mind. Meme' had told him what the word *'quickening'* meant.

She said that it was when the Spirit of God breathed on a word, or words, that had been received and planted inside of us, and they came alive for some purpose in the heart. She said that if we cared for those words, like precious seeds, rather than ignoring them, plants would grow, and, in God's timing: fruit. She had told him that, no doubt that was what God had done in him.

Though it wasn't exactly a good *feeling*, he was happy to hear that the LORD had spoken to him. He knew that he had been privileged. Since that time he had felt a burden to donate what he could to help out with Mr. Jack's project. He didn't often get money, but it was surprising how little was needed to accomplish something. It was clear, even to Josiah that money amongst the Kurdistan people stretched further than it did in the United States. He always felt good about his giving and was ever trying to come up with plans and ways to make some money for these people whom he had never met and who seemed to live in his heart.

He loved the way Mr. Jack called them an ancient people. That sounded so honorable.

Chapter One

School Days

As far as Josiah was concerned, it had been forever since he had seen his friends from out west. A year was such a long time, especially to a boy of nearly ten. Oh, he had kept in touch with Mr. Jack, but email wasn't the same as seeing him face-to-face.

The truth was, if someone had asked Josiah who his closest friend was outside his immediate family and church group, he would have named Jack Harris, and Mr. Jack was old enough to be his grandfather.

Now, normally he would have called someone like Mr. Jack, Mr. Harris, or Pastor Harris, but Mr. Jack himself had insisted that Josiah call him Jack. Josiah couldn't quite bring himself to do that, so they settled for 'Mr. Jack'. That worked for both of them.

The year before, Josiah had spent some time on a ranch in Colorado with Jack, his wife Patty, and their son Peter. He liked Mrs. Patty and Pete very much. He and Pete had become buddies right off. Pete seemed to know how to talk with kids without making them feel like they didn't know anything.

Josiah listened attentively every time he heard any news announced in church about his friend Mr. Jack going to Iraq or whatever he might be doing. Mr. Jack had a mission outreach project out there in the Mideast that ministered to the Kurdistan people, a people who could trace their roots back to the most ancient history.

These people had been displaced by Saddam Hussein and his men and basically had no place to call their own. Many of the women were left as widows when their husbands were savagely annihilated by Hussein, leaving behind many children with no fathers.

Once when Mr. Jack had preached in his church he showed the pictures of these women and children and how they lived. Josiah had wept. He just couldn't hold it back. He didn't feel too badly about crying though, because, even as Mr. Jack had shared their story and pictures at the conference, he had cried too. As a matter of fact, Josiah thought that maybe there hadn't been a dry eye in the church.

But when Josiah had left the church that day and throughout the whole next day, he just couldn't get the Kurdistan people out of his mind. Meme' had told him what the word *'quickening'* meant.

She said that it was when the Spirit of God breathed on a word, or words that had been received and planted inside of us, and they came alive for some purpose in the heart. She said that if we cared for those words, like precious seeds, rather than ignoring them, plants would grow, and, in God's timing: fruit. She had told him that, no doubt that was what God had done in him.

Though it wasn't exactly a good *feeling*, he was happy to hear that the LORD had spoken to him. He knew that he had been privileged. Since that time he had felt a burden to donate what he could to help out with Mr. Jack's project. He didn't often get money, but it was surprising how little was needed to accomplish something. It was clear, even to Josiah that money amongst the Kurdistan people stretched further than it did in the United States. He always felt good about his giving and was ever trying to come up with plans and ways to make some money for these people whom he had never met and who seemed to live in his heart.

Josiah came from a family of seven children. He was second in line. Needless to say, there was no such thing as extra money in his house, though, for sure, God took good care of his family.

He had a good life; full of adventure, love, and many people who cared for him greatly. He enjoyed it very much and knew that he had so many things to be thankful for. He and his older brother Zachary had had many adventures together. They thrived on them and had come to know that life itself was an adventure.

They lived in a wooded area in the country with much to do, especially if you were a boy with an imagination. They had a big pond on their property, down the hill in front of his grandparents' home. They lived just a stone's throw away from Pepe' and Meme', and the children wandered in and out of both houses freely.

On normal weekdays Josiah and Zachary saw their cousins, Cameron and Christopher every day as they went to school together. Their grandmother, Meme' was their teacher, so they spent much time together. These two cousins were their closest friends. Though they didn't like to admit it, they were glad to see Mondays roll around so they could get together. Actually all four of them felt the same.

The companionship of their buddies made school much more tolerable for all of them, but especially, it seemed, for Josiah, who was the youngest of the four boys. His mind would wander during class periods in particular now that the weather was getting warmer, and he thought of so many things he could be doing instead of sitting in a classroom studying.

After all, there were forts and rafts just waiting to be built. There were woods to be explored and discoveries to be made, fish to be caught, and stones to be skipped across the surface of the glistening water. There was a boat that needed rowing, trees and rocks to be climbed, bikes to be ridden, tents waiting to be set up; animals practically begging him to come out and sneak up on them. And what of the hoops crying out from the sports field waiting for basketballs? How could even a good day in school compare with any day outside?

Once he had heard Pepe' say that he felt all the kids should be allowed to play outside, enjoying their youth before it got away from them. He said they would want to learn when they were older and that it would be so much easier on everyone; that is, the teachers and their pupils. Pepe', of course, was only joking, and, I suppose that his grandchildren knew it, but Josiah thought it was a good idea. He liked Pepe'.

He had been told many times by the adults in his life that one day he would be thankful for the time he had spent in school and the efforts he had put forth to learn, but so far he had not entirely believed it, for it was so outside anything that he could comprehend. He had tried once to convince Meme' and his mother, Jackie, that they should have science every afternoon, and go out exploring. He thought it was a great plan. He knew the other boys did too, though they didn't open their mouths to back him up when they saw how he was struggling, trying to convince them. Neither Meme' nor his mother had been willing to go along with it.

Chapter Two

The Brainstorm

It was Friday morning and Josiah was thrilled that the weekend was ahead of them. If he had to go to school, he thought, Friday, was the day he liked best. It was late in the school year, so he knew that it wouldn't be long before he would be free for the summer.

Cameron, Christopher, and their seven-year-old sister Tabitha had arrived for school. The day began as any other normal school day. Because it was Friday, they had their weekly spelling test. Josiah had studied and was determined that he wasn't going to miss any words. He always felt good when he 'aced' a test. If he had to go to school, he had decided, at least he would do well. The thought of repeating a grade was more frightening than any punishment he could think of; it was not even to be considered. He had thoroughly ruled it out even as a possibility.

Instead of their usual work during English period, Meme' assigned the boys, all but Cameron who was in high school that is, a composition on what they wanted to do this summer.

"Brainstorm," she told them. "You don't have to rush; in fact I don't want you to. Take your time and think about it. Don't discuss it amongst yourselves though. I want your own ideas."

And so, you see, that is what Josiah was trying to do: brainstorm. He knew he wouldn't get away with simply writing that he wanted to spend the summer outside. Not only would he get a failing grade, but he would have to do it over anyway. Meme' was tough on them in that way. She didn't let her students get away with much, or, at least that's what Josiah felt. He loved his Meme' though, and knew that she loved him too.

He noticed that Zach was already busy at work. His pencil was gliding across the paper as though he had come to school knowing that that would be their assignment. Christopher was just as Josiah was; staring at the paper.

Josiah turned and looked out the solid wall of windows that faced the pond in front of the house. He tried to keep his mind on task, but could almost see himself out in the boat that was anchored by the dock. His eyes swept to the right to the field where they spent so much time. Several times Pepe' and Meme' had held a summer jamboree there for the church. They were the senior pastors and Josiah's father and mother, Rob and Jackie, were the assistant pastors. All the children in the church were very much a part of Josiah's life. He had many friends.

He could imagine, as he daydreamed; I mean: *brainstormed,* the times that Mr. Jack and Mrs. Patty camped out there too. They seemed to like the outdoors very much, and, both said that they enjoyed their time in the tents more than those times they had spent in motels.

He recalled when there had been a big thunderstorm and Mr. Jack was in the tent alone. He had been tired and said that he would go and rest a while.

The rains had come down in a torrent; heavy, and for a long time, they beat upon the canvas. The sky had gotten very dark, especially for the middle of the afternoon, and that, so quickly. Thunder pealed with a vengeance and the lightning seemed to be showing off as it flashed and bolted, lighting up the dark skies.

Josiah had been worried about Mr. Jack. He knew that he wouldn't make a run for the house with the rain coming down so heavily.

After the storm, Mr. Jack came up to the house with a big smile on his face. Most of the storm, he told them, he had slept through. And, when he did wake, he enjoyed it so much. That was what Josiah liked most about Mr. Jack. He was so full of adventure.

"Josiah," Meme' interrupted his thoughts. "Come on. You're supposed to be writing."

"I'm brainstorming, Meme'," quipped back Josiah, smiling.

The truth is though, that Josiah had been brainstorming without realizing it. As he looked at his paper again, ideas began to pop into his mind for what he would like to do during the summer. He began to write and it seemed his pencil could not keep up with his thoughts. He liked it when that happened. Meme' said that was inspiration.

He noticed that Chris had not begun to write. He was still staring at his paper. Quickly Josiah came to the conclusion that that proved his point; daydreaming was a good thing. It would have been better he thought, if Chris had taken a little time to look out the window and had allowed his imagination to kick in at the beautiful distractions that were waiting out there. Maybe an idea would have come to him from something he saw or remembered. He went back to his writing.

In no time it seemed, he filled one side of his paper and turned it over. Meme' had to smile for she couldn't recall ever seeing him write with such fervor.

"Can we use more than one sheet of paper, Meme?" he asked.

"Certainly," she answered. Clearly he was 'on a roll' and she had no intention of trying to stop him. She would have said that it was rare footage to view Josiah and writing as friends. He wrote until lunch time. Handwriting was not Josiah's strongpoint and it took him some time as he filled almost three sheets of paper.

Finally, he finished to his satisfaction.

"Meme," he said, handing her his work, "You said that this was a composition, right? Are you going to mark us down for penmanship, spelling, and punctuation, or just what's in it?

"This is English, Josiah," she answered. "Of course you must know that everything counts."

Because of the exceptional content of his paper, Meme' felt she needed to be graciously lenient on that which would normally have brought his grade down. She didn't want to stifle his creative juices, as clearly his work had been inspired, and even he seemed to know it.

"This is a great paper, Josiah," she said; to which comment he beamed from one end to the other. "It is the finest composition you have written. It is full of good ideas and I will read it to the class, unless, of course, you would like to read it yourself."

"No, Meme'," he answered shyly. "Will you?"

He was pleased, of course, with the praise, and happy to have the others hear it. They listened intently.

"Wow!" said Zach, not slack to give his brother praise, "that's great, Siah. I thought my paper was good, but it doesn't compare with yours."

"That's OK," Meme' broke in, "It's not a competition."

When the school day was done, Meme' got onto the computer and typed an email to her friend Jack Harris. She wanted to share with him what Josiah had written in his composition. She knew that he would be pleased.

She had no intention of telling Josiah that she sent it to Jack. She would let that information come out between the two of them.

Chapter Three

The Wilderness

Out in the state of Washington Jack Harris sat at his computer and opened the email from his New England friend, Val, Josiah's Meme'. It was marked, "Josiah's Composition". The longer he knew Josiah, the more he liked him. He was a neat kid with a tender heart. Jack wished more adults had a heart like his.

Val wrote that she had tried to keep it as close to original as she could, but for the grammar, punctuation, and spelling errors. Jack laughed as he thought that she could probably have left it in its original condition and he may not have even noticed the errors. The point she wanted to make had only to do with the content of his composition. He read it thoroughly. In his mind's eye he could picture his young friend's face and enthusiasm.

WHAT I WANT TO DO THIS SUMMER

By: Josiah James Beauchene

This summer I would like to see my friend Jack Harris. I think I have a good idea that might help the people in Northern Iraq.

The people in our church are always trying to come up with ways to raise a little money for the Kurdistan people who sometimes don't even have enough food for their families. Many of them don't even get to see a doctor, no matter what is wrong with them. It is not like it is over here for children. Even if someone is poor they can usually get food and go to see a doctor in this country.

Jack Harris told us one time that he wished people over here could understand what the culture was like in the Mideast, compared with our own. He said it was amazing how they were satisfied with so little. He told us that their culture had not changed much from what it was like in Biblical times.

I love the way he calls them an ancient people. That sounds so honorable. Some of them eat the same food every day, without any change, but, Mr. Jack said, they don't seem to mind. They are just happy to be able to have food to give to their families.

Many of them live in small shelters, which aren't really like houses at all, and they are crowded with many people living and sleeping in one tiny room. I know it is true because Mr. Jack showed us some slides and even some videos about them.

My Meme' is older than many of the women over there, but they look so much older than she does. And, they look sad and very tired.

A while ago I heard a sermon in church about the Jewish people leaving Egypt at the time of the Exodus. You can read it in the Bible if you want to. It comes right after Genesis.

They spent forty years in the wilderness as they walked to the Promised Land. Forty years is a very long time to live in tents. We went to Florida once in the van and it took three days. We thought we were never going to get there. They ate manna every day and wore the same shoes for forty years that never wore out, because the LORD was taking care of them.

Meme' taught us about seven special places they stopped on their way to the Promised Land. I thought *it was very interesting and I wish I could remember the name of even one of the places, but I can't.*

Since Mr. Jack would like the people over here to understand the way the people over there live, and their culture that goes back so many years, I have a good idea for a great adventure.

I thought it might be nice if Mr. Jack, Mrs. Patty, and their son Pete led a tour group of boys, since they like them so much and are so good with them, across a wilderness out west in a place where there are no houses and no paved roads. If he thought it out, I know that he could do it, because he's really smart and Meme' says he's great at planning things out and making them work.

It would be nice if it was a forty day trip: but that would probably be too long; maybe three weeks would be better. Everyone could tent out at night; bring only one pair of shoes and not too many clothes to change into.

We could build (here Jack noticed the change to "we" instead of "they") *a fire every night. Ahead of time, Mr. Jack and his team could set up the seven special places to stop, like those Meme' told us about.*

Mr. Jack could be like Moses as he led the people, only the people would want to be with him instead of giving him a lot of trouble and acting rebelliously.

Along the way he could tell stories by the campfire from the Bible or from his experiences with the Mid Eastern people. Pete could play his guitar while everyone sang. Everyone would learn so much. We (there it was again) could eat the same foods every day without all the variety we usually have, and drink only water. Everyone would have to agree ahead of time that no one could complain or they wouldn't be able to come. It would be very much like the story in Exodus and the life of the Kurdistan people today.

Mr. Jack could charge people to bring them on this tour and I think they would be happy to pay for the experience. We could take along some pack animals like donkeys or mules to carry all the things. It would be fun and I don't think anyone who went would ever forget it. I know I wouldn't.

And that is what I would like to do this summer. And I would like it if Zach, Cameron, and Chris, could come with me. We would have fun.

"Well, doesn't he beat all," Jack murmured to himself. He was humbled by Josiah's confidence in him for, truth be known, he didn't feel even to be named in the same sentence with the great prophet Moses.

One of the dogs came over to his feet to see if he were being summoned. Jack reached down to scratch the dog between its ears and the dog leaned against his knee. "I don't know," he said, as though running it by the dog, "sure sounds like a lot of work to me. Still, it might be fun."

"What's that, Jack?" asked Patty as she was passing through the room; her arms full of clean clothes to be put away. "I didn't hear what you said."

"Oh, I guess I was talking to myself," he said. "Come read this, Patty. See what you think. It's a school paper from Val that Josiah did today for English. It'll speak for itself. Here, sit down," he said as he rose from the chair to let his wife sit.

She plunked down, happy for the change in her activity. And, she read.

Chapter Four

Man's Best Friend

Jack stood by while his wife Patty read Josiah's composition. "So, who's going to help you with this project and when do we go, you old softy?" she asked, chuckling.

She really didn't expect an answer as she rose to continue putting the clean wash away for it was simply one of those rhetorical questions.

Jack sat back down and began to feed information through his search engine. Patty did not as much as glance back to see what he might be looking into. She figured he would be researching whatever *it* was for the rest of the day, and, more than likely she was right, for she knew her husband's ways pretty well. And, he knew by her comment that the project had her approval.

As he surfed here and there, he thought about last year's trip to Colorado and the great time he had had, guiding the tours across the range and up into the mountains. It had been a fun summer, and seemed to be the fastest on record. While the boys had gotten much out of it, he knew that he had been even more blessed. That was so God's way, he thought. Not only was it a great boost for the project in Iraq, but he, Patty, and Pete had come back with many great memories.

But still, three weeks is a long time, he thought, not just for him but for a large group of active boys.

He sure could use a little time off though. It had been a difficult year of going back and forth to the Mideast, to say nothing of the travel in his own country. He noticed that the older he got, the harder it was on him. Oh, he wasn't complaining; he enjoyed his calling, but it was not an easy one.

Leading an exodus across the wilderness wouldn't exactly be time off, he told himself.

But still, it would be a nice break from the routine and his wife could go with him. He wasn't sure how

Pete would feel about it, but his son certainly had fun last year, and had really been in his element. It would be good therapy for all of them.

Now this type of thinking was what Mr. Jack would have called 'reasoning with himself'; weighing the pros and cons. He did it all the time when something new presented itself. It seemed to him the right and only thing to do and it came as natural as breathing to him. He certainly didn't want to jump into anything blindly, and, if it was going to be some sort of group effort; how could he convince others on it if he were not sold out himself?

You see, Mr. Jack was a passionate man who did not like to do things half-heartedly. He could barely function in a lukewarm climate. His unspoken rule, in those areas where he did have a choice, was that something be ruled out or that he should be sold out. He did not like standing on middle ground.

As he typed and searched, sipping his cup of coffee, he patted the dog, who was back to play its part in the decision making. "Well, pooch" he said to the dog again, "Do I talk myself into it, or out of it? What do you think?"

He paused for a moment to read what had come up on the screen, and then looked back at 'man's best friend'. "That's what I thought. You don't even have an opinion one way or the other, do you? Well, this is some fine mess you've gotten us into." He snickered at the nonsense of his own train of thought and conversation. It looked to him like maybe the dog might have been chuckling with him, but you never knew with this dog. The stinker might have been laughing *at* him; not *with* him. He liked his dogs. They were good listeners and not very critical. Oh, once in a while they might cop an attitude, but, they could be quickly talked out of it. For the most part though, they were his buddies. Back to his computer he turned. "Why don't you get back over there in the corner," he suggested to the dog, "I've got work to do and you're holding me up."

The dog let out a little sigh, barely audible, and, seeming to understand its master, sulked its way back to the corner, lay on the rug, and closed its eyes.

When he was satisfied with his cyber search, Jack determined to make some phone calls. He had many acquaintances out west, and he was interested in their take on the project. Before he made any calls at all, however, he moved over to a more comfortable chair with what was left of his coffee, to talk it over with the LORD. He would not attempt to do anything without discussing it with Him. Oh, he would do his research, but make no effort in finalizing a single thing without feeling that he had the mind of God to do it.

As soon as he sat down the dog came over again.

"I'm going to pray," he said to his companion. "Leave me alone for a while." After praying for some time he picked up his Bible to read a few passages that he felt the LORD had quickened to his spirit. They were not exactly 'writing on the wall' passages, but they brought peace to him that God, in fact, was in control.

He would continue going forward and believe that at any time, if God did not want him to move ahead, He had not only the power to stop him, but Jack's permission. Hadn't he prayed after all, "LORD, if it is your will for us to do this thing, then, open the door and let no man close it? And, if not, Father, then close the door with the force of heaven that no man, not even me, can open it."

When he walked back to his desk to make those calls he felt very contented and, at peace. He did not always feel that way, though, for certain he wanted to, but right now he did. He knew that God had heard his prayer and would have His way. That felt good.

"Come on over here," he said to the dog that seemed to be pretending to be asleep now. Quickly the old dog stood and wagged its tail as it did whenever it felt the honor of having been summoned.

He rubbed the dog's head again, between the ears where it liked it most. "You're a good mutt, my friend," he said, "though you can be a bit moody. We old curmudgeons have to stick together."

He picked up the phone and went back to his work; Jack, I mean; not the dog.

Chapter Five

The Plot Thickens

About two weeks later Josiah received a letter from his Washington friend. It had been attached to an email addressed to Josiah's mother and father asking them to read it first. When Jackie called him into the house she had a big smile on her face.

He could barely contain himself when he knew it was from Mr. Jack. He sat to read his mail but in no way did he connect it with the paper that he had written. Anything that had happened two weeks ago had been quickly filed in the back of his mind, maybe for another time and, maybe not.

Let the reader here not misunderstand, for when Josiah wrote the paper it was not about an assignment or a grade, though he had gotten an A. No, it was about an idea that he had to help the Kurdistan people and he felt that it was a good one. And that's all it was. That he received a good grade was so much the better.

Up until this time he had no idea that Meme' had even mailed a copy of it to Mr. Jack. But, as always, he was excited to hear from his friend.

He was a good reader and dived right into it. In his mind's eye, he could almost see his friend sitting across from him at the desk and could hear his voice.

Hey there Josiah,

How's my mission partner? Everyone here is fine. Patty and Pete asked me to send their love and big hugs your way. I tried to tell them that cowboys don't hug that regular, but they would hear none of it nor would they listen but insisted that I send them anyway. So I send you their hugs so they won't be offended and at the same time I might as well throw in one or two from me.

Your Meme' sent me a copy of a composition you wrote a couple of weeks ago. You sure can come up with the ideas. Man, what did I do before you came along?

We have decided upon a few things. First, we are not doing the trail with Mustgofast again this year. It was great and that doesn't mean we won't do it again, but, I feel like something new might be beneficial to help fund the work in Iraq and to offer ministry in the states as well. Apparently, by your paper, you feel it too. Who knows, maybe some of the boys who came last year might be able to make it again this year with the help of some support from the church folks.

I have been working feverishly, as you have waited so late in the year to come up with your plan. (It's probably your Meme's fault for not assigning it sooner. Let's blame her!) As you know, it is almost summertime, and if I'm going to do this thing I need to put it into action. The wheels are already turning though. I have been in touch with several people that I know in Colorado and they think your plan is great. Our expense wouldn't be much, for I know a man with a great parcel of land who will allow us to use it for our Exodus program. He has put at our disposal his donkeys and mules.

We have decided to do as you wrote; that is to run it for three weeks. Along the way we will eat mainly beans, beef jerky, barrel pickles, coffee, water, and sourdough bread. We will have beans for breakfast, lunch, and supper. (Remember the beans we had on the trail last year? Man, were they good! Don't know how I'll feel about three weeks' worth though.) There will be no marshmallows toasted over the fire, my young friend, and no chocolate milk. (Woe is me?! This is a revolting development. Thanks a lot, Josiah!)

Like last year's trek, those who come will be limited by the list we send out. They will need a pair of high leather boots; you remember the snakes out there, a backpack with limited accessories such as soap, shampoo, toothbrushes, toothpaste, sunscreen, and deodorant. (I don't know why we should have to bring along those things. It's not like girls are going to be there, other than Patty, but for some reason she insists on it. I tried to tell her that I doubt whether the Israelites brought all those incidentals, but she would hear none of it. She can be pretty stubborn that way and sometimes downright cantankerous, so we better humor her. I wouldn't want her mad at me from the start. That just would not do. Man that would make for a mighty long three weeks.) Josiah had to stop and laugh here, for Mr. Jack had put in a winking smiley face. *And, of course everyone needs a Bible.*

A list of particular items of clothing, including a cowboy hat and kerchief, and the amount of each piece allowed will be sent out. There will be no exceptions. Everyone has to make it work, just like in the days of the great Exodus; it **must** *work because there will be no going back.*

The trip will begin on the last week in June and go for three weeks, as I said; no, as you said.

Everyone will need a tent, just like last year, either for one or two sleepers, and a sleeping bag. We will have a small supply wagon for our foodstuffs and pack animals as you suggested. Everyone will walk. We have already begun to map out the trail. I am studying the seven major stopping places. Your Meme' has made it hard on me with all this studying, but I think she enjoys that. (Josiah knew that Mr. Jack was joking. Josiah loved his sense of humor and how he always picked on Meme'.)

The reason I am giving you all this information is that I have asked your mother if you could come. Of course, I cannot manage it without you. After all, the idea is yours. You have to foot some of the responsibility you know. You cannot just come up with these bright ideas and drop them into someone's lap expecting not to help out. Anyhow Pete has me 'over a barrel' for he has told me he won't come if you're not there. Isn't that like some kind of evil manipulation? I went along with it though because he's so sensitive about it. He will bring his guitar, of course.

And, oh, I can't see how we can manage without your three school buddies, Zach, Cameron, and Christopher either.

Because the plan was yours we will pay for your flights as well as the tickets for the other three. I have called many of the church pastors to run the idea by them and their people. It was received with excitement, and not just from the boys.

I am certain that it will be a wonderful learning experience for everyone, including the adults. We will pray for a big turnout as I have many adults willing to volunteer so that they might come along if the crowd is big.

And, let's believe God for great resources for Iraq!

Mr. Jack signed it and said that he would be in touch as further plans came together. His letter sounded as though he was excited about the whole thing.

"Mom," said Josiah, choking a little with emotion, "can we go?"

"Yes, you may," she said as she hugged this sensitive son. "Dad and I talked it over and we think it would be a wonderful thing. Three weeks seems like a long time though," she said, wiping a tear from her cheek.

He hugged his mother to comfort her, of course, though a tear or two threatened to betray him. He couldn't wait for school the following day to talk to Uncle Dalton, Cameron and Christopher's father, about whether the boys could come with them. He didn't want to talk on the phone. He wanted to see the looks on their faces.

Just then Zach came up the stairs. Their mother and Josiah both turned to look at him. "What?" he said, almost defensively; feeling a little guilty though he had done nothing wrong.

Both of them laughed. It seemed to break the heaviness of the thought of being separated for so long.

They knew they would both be fine and the time would go quickly.

"Hey, Zach," began Josiah, "Remember that composition I wrote. Meme' sent it to Mr. Jack and he's going to do it. We're going to Colorado for three weeks. Cameron and Christopher get to come with us if their mother and father let them!"

The expression on Zach's face was priceless as he looked absolutely dumbfounded.

"Didn't I tell you it was a great composition, Siah?" he asked his younger brother. Wow! We're going to Colorado again! Are you going to call Cameron and Chris?"

"No," his mother answered quickly. "And don't you say anything. Siah will tell them the news himself when they come for school tomorrow morning."

The two boys headed down for the pond, unimpressed now, it seemed, by the plans they had made that afternoon for boating and fishing. But, they went anyway.

Chapter Six

By Popular Demand

Here I will write what the reader most likely has already surmised. Cameron and Christopher were excited about the trip, as were their father and mother. They had not gone with Siah and Zach to Colorado the previous year, and so they were doubly thrilled, never having done anything that compared with this.

Meme' said it was a good thing this whole string of events came up at the end of the school year, or, for certain, they would all be repeating a grade beginning in the fall. Their work was inadequate and there had not been much of it. It had been a major task to make it through all of the preoccupation with the upcoming trip.

She understood though, but, in her own words, "Just because I understand is not to say that it is alright."

About a week after Mr. Jack's email Josiah received the printed brochure that was being sent out to the different churches around to distribute for information and advertising. When he opened it the boys were all standing around him, for they had been enjoying their last day of school. What great timing!

The front of the brochure caused each of them to 'ooh and ah'. It was vividly beautiful, the colors fairly jumping off the page. The background was a breathtaking scenic photo of the Colorado landscape.

The fact is the attraction of the brochure can simply not be appropriately represented by words alone, for truly, in this case, even as the cliché goes, "A picture is worth a thousand words".

It was obvious that someone had not only been talented, but inspired. It would be hard to imagine that any young man's eyes could pass by it and not be drawn to at least check out the brochure's contents.

Zach concluded that Mr. Jack must have done the work himself, for he was an expert with photography, a field that Zach and his dad also enjoyed very much. Last year they had seen some of his professional movies for his project in Iraq. They were remarkable.

In the foreground was last year's photo of Josiah with Mustgofast: the now famous mustang with his boy. Beneath the photo was a caption that read:

Mission Inspired by: Josiah James Beauchene

And, on the top in simple lettering:

...BACK BY POPULAR DEMAND...
JACK HARRIS TOURS

And, on the bottom:

STOPPING PLACES

A three-week Exodus experience for Young Men
Ages: 10-18yrs.

The inside, of course, contained particulars about the trip and contact information. There was a special invitation to the many boys who had been part of last year's tour. Because of the loan of the pack animals and the land area, and the necessary voluntary assistants who actually sounded like they wanted to go, Mr. Jack was pleased to announce that all of that would help to keep the price down and hopefully affordable. He homed in on the facet of the trip that was not simply gleaning funds for the Mideast project, but developing a healthy burden and appreciation for that ancient culture and our own godly heritage. Of course he also mentioned the fun of the adventure that lay before those who came.

Though it seemed the time would never pass and the day to leave would always be just a dream, slightly out of their reach, finally the day in fact, did arrive. It was a Sunday. The boys had been in church for part of the service to say their goodbyes to everyone, and then to head for the airport. Anyone might have guessed where they were going for they all wore blue jeans, western shirts, hats, high cowboy boots, and big smiles.

Of course the church prayed for them for safe travel, going and returning, health, the blessing of a great experience with much fruit for them individually and for the Kurdistan people of Iraq, and even that they would not become homesick. It was a good time of prayer and each of the boys was moved by it. They liked their church.

All four of the parents were happy that the boys were going together for each knew that alone any one of them might have been more than a little homesick. They felt that it might grip them in particular at nighttime, but the support of the others would help them weather those periods.

"Remember their testimonies when they returned last year?" Pepe' asked the folks in the church. "They said they dropped into bed so tired that they couldn't stay awake to be homesick. And, the days were almost too busy to even think about home."

The two fathers, Rob and Dalton, took the boys to the airport. The mothers hugged their sons and said their farewells in the church parking lot, then walked back in to be a part of the rest of the service. The parents had decided it would be better for everyone that way, as they would have had to take two vehicles to the airport.

Cameron and Christopher had never flown and both were very excited to be going by plane. They felt a certain security in the fact that Josiah and Zach had flown several times and were familiar with the 'ins and outs' of the whole flight experience. Besides that, because of their youth, one of the flight attendants was responsible to keep an eye out for them. Once in the plane, they had nothing to concern themselves over, for the flight was direct and someone would be meeting them at the airport.

For a time the boys looked out the window of the plane, but soon they grew sleepy. They talked for a while, and then leaned back in their seats, but eventually each of them fell asleep.

In no time at all, the pilot announced that they would soon be landing in Denver. None of the boys could fathom it, but, believe me when I tell you that they were all excited that the time had passed so rapidly.

The veteran travelers, Josiah and Zach, briefed their cousins about what would more than likely be happening. It was late afternoon when they arrived, though two hours later at home. They had all slept so they were raring to go. When they walked into the airport Jack and Patty were there to greet them; looking as excited as the boys felt.

They all hugged and exchanged greetings. "Hey," asked Josiah, "Where's the handsome Harris?" He and Zach laughed as they remembered how Pete had first introduced himself to them. They had both liked him immediately.

"He's out in the van waiting for us," said Mr. Jack. "Only two of us were allowed in here because of Homeland Security."

Mr. Jack took the time to muss Josiah's hair. It was clear he was very happy to see all the boys. He would have said that it brought the 'boy' out in him, and all of them would probably have agreed.

"Hungry?" Patty asked in her straightforward, easy-to-respond-to way, "Man, I'm starved! We waited for you boys figuring maybe they didn't give you any food on the plane." Several times last year Zach and Josiah had talked about her and how easy it would be to call her Aunt Patty. They would have been proud to add her to their list of aunts. They had more aunts and uncles, great aunts and great uncles than they knew of. Their father and mother both came from large extended families and there was no want for relatives.

Zachary and Josiah were the first to respond as they had lost their shyness about such things, at least amongst these friends, the previous year. Almost in unison they answered, "Yah, starved!

"How about you two?" asked Mr. Jack, referring of course to Cameron and Christopher. Both of them gave a little shyer answer, but clearly everyone was very hungry. How could boys that age not be, unless, of course, they were sick?

In the meantime Mr. Jack had called Pete to meet them at the curbside with the van. He was all smiles as he jumped out, not only to help, but to greet his old buddies with hugs and to meet Cameron and Chris.

"Man, is anyone as hungry as I am?" he asked as they piled into the van. And then, "What's so funny?" This kinda' hunger is nothing to laugh about."

"Remember where we stopped last year?" Mr. Jack asked Josiah and Zach.

"Yes," Josiah answered quickly, "near Boulder."

Mr. Jack was impressed. Either he had studied up before he came, or he had an excellent memory. "I remember because the name was like a big rock, and because the food was so great. Zach and I talked at home and hoped that we could stop at the same place. We really liked it."

Zach flushed a little red now, clearly embarrassed, but he knew that Siah was pretty straight forward and didn't see any harm in blurting out these things. Zach knew it wouldn't make a bit of difference to talk to Josiah about it, because he just didn't see what the big deal was and what was so private about conversations like that. "After all, it's just food," he would have said, "and everyone has to eat, Zach".

Zach could have saved himself some anxiety if he knew how Josiah's openness endeared the Harris's all the more to him. There was no reason to be embarrassed or to feel he had something to apologize for.

"Then, Boulder it is," said Mr. Jack.

"How far is it to the Exodus place, Mr. Jack?" continued Josiah. "Is it anywhere near Longmont where we went last year?"

"Well it's between Longmont and Fort Collins," he answered. "We should be there in less than two hours; it's not such a long ride. The area is very mountainous, but also has some flats and some range land. There are plenty of caves and streams. It's not exactly authentic Sinai Peninsula, but we're not trying to duplicate the terrain anyway. It's more about the experience, right?"

All the boys agreed with him for they understood Josiah's vision clearly. They had talked it over so much since Mr. Jack's email that they had all gotten caught up in it and shared Josiah's burden.

It's hard to say if they were more excited last year or this, for at this time last year Josiah and Zachary were a little unsure of themselves in this unfamiliar territory and with a group they really didn't know that well. This year was different though; they were with old friends, not just acquaintances. You cannot compare the two.

Chapter Seven

Passing By

"There's the diner!" shouted Josiah to the boys. He recognized it by the longhorns and the hitching post in the front.

"And, I remember they have the best cheeseburgers around," added Zach. "Man, are they great!"

"And the fries are good, too, added Pete. Come on, let's go. What are we waiting for?" he said with mock impatience trying to loosen up Cameron and Chris as both of them seemed a little unsure about voicing an opinion.

"Hope you boys like cheeseburgers," Patty said to the two as they were walking in, "because if you do, you're in for a treat."

After wolfing down their lunch the group headed north. "You were right," said Cameron, "those burgers were the best."

"I can't believe how fast I finished them," added Chris, who, under normal circumstances would have been the last of the boys to finish eating. These, however, were not normal circumstances. He had been famished. He couldn't remember the last time he had been so hungry when he sat down to eat. "I guess flying makes you hungry," he concluded, not really allowing for the fact that he had only had a small breakfast and back at home it was two hours later.

There had been little conversation around the table as all of them were eager to get on their way. The official start of the ***Stopping Places*** wilderness trek was tomorrow.

"How many are coming, Mr. Jack?" asked Josiah.

"Well, thanks to your bright idea Josiah you've gotten us into another mess this year." There was that Harris humor again. Josiah loved it. Actually, all the boys did. "We had more register than we knew what to do with. Even our highest guess didn't come close to the numbers that applied. Since I sent the pamphlets to all the churches on the same day, we felt the only fair way to do it was 'first come; first serve'. We did make an exception for one of the boys who wanted to come, but was unsure as to whether he could come up with the money. It didn't seem fair to leave him out because he certainly wasn't dragging his feet.

Many of the boys from last summer will be here too. One of the planning team suggested leaving them out to give the others a chance, but, in thinking it over and talking to the LORD about it, that isn't right. If they are really aggressive and quick to respond to these things, it doesn't seem right to leave them out. God has allowed me to do many things in my own life. I would hate to feel that I would be left out next time, just because someone else needs a turn. That is not God's way; in some areas; yes, but in this; no. I'm sure you boys know that. Remember what Matthew said, 'For whoever has to him shall be given, and he shall have more abundance.' I'm so glad that God does things His way.

Anyway, in answer to your question, I gave a lot of thought to the numbers and planned carefully. We have one hundred, twenty boys coming and twelve teams of chaperones besides Patty, Pete, and me. The three of us count as one. That makes, of course, twelve groups of twelve each. All of the team leaders are married couples except for one. Pete knows of a man from around this area who has been a widower for about five years. He's retired and is a good man and very active in his local church.

When his pastor read the brochure to his church the man called Pete to ask if it might be possible that he could go as a leader. A note had been sent in the flyer that ideally the leaders would be married couples coming as a team with references from their pastors.

It seems he sort of lost direction when his wife died. Oh, he is still following the LORD, but doesn't seem to have the joy and satisfaction from it that he used to. He feels that something is wrong because he knows the promises of God to those who follow Him. He hopes this trip might help him find his way back to that joy.

Of all the leaders, Random Mann, that's the man's name, is the only one I don't know. It's enough that Pete and the fellow's pastor recommended him. That works for us. All the others are from churches where I've preached and, actually, I know all of them; some only casually, and others, quite well. I'm certain that it will do Random much good to spend three weeks with you boys. I know it sure helped me last year in areas that I didn't even know I needed help, but God, the Good Father knew it. He takes care of His sons and daughters and knows what we need.

By the way, I want to bring up another thing here, along the same line." The boys were all ears and very much into the conversation. "We weren't sure if you boys wanted to be part of mine and Patty's team or if you prefer to go with another chaperone. You won't hurt our feelings if you want to go with someone else for any reason. We figured the four of you would want to stay together and we put you in our team because Josiah is as much a part of the hub of this as I am. Well, what do you think?"

All four boys smiled at the idea of Mr. Jack and Mrs. Patty wanting them in the leadership team. That was exciting to them. "How about Pete?" asked Josiah.

"Actually he'll hang out helping where he's needed, especially with our team. Pete, Patty, and I officially make up one leader. Random will be the other in charge of the Levites. It should work out well that way, I think. It will give us all a little spare time as I will have a lot of planning and other work to do as well. Of course, more or less, Patty and I will be responsible for the four of you boys.

Josiah and Zachary both noticed the turn that led in the direction of the ranch where Mustgofast was kept. "Didn't we just pass by the road where Mustgofast lives?" asked Josiah.

"Yes, we did," answered Mr. Jack. "You're really observant there, Siah."

Josiah thought to himself, "How can anyone possibly forget where one of their best friends lives."

For a time his mood dipped down at the thought of being so close to the mustang and not being able to stop, and everyone picked up on it. Pete jumped in to continue the conversation and to help lift up Josiah.

"So," Pete said, "I wonder what great adventure is waiting for us this year. I don't know about the rest of you, but this comes at a good time for me. I'm really excited." Immediately Josiah was drawn back into the conversation. If there was one language that he understood clearly it was the language of adventure.

"We're going to have more than just one adventure," he stated loudly, and very sure of himself. "I know we are."

"There goes the positive prophet," Jack thought, "You just gotta' love that kid. He's like a good medicine when something ails you."

When they had left the restaurant Mr. Jack had taken over the driving. Pete was sitting in the back seat of the ten-passenger van and grabbed for his guitar. "Hey, boys," he said. "Let's sing a few tunes," and he began to play.

The songs he played were familiar to everyone and all of them joined in the singing.

Chapter Eight

Anticipation

In no time it seemed, they arrived at the place set for the meeting of all who would come. It appeared that already most of the boys and the leaders had arrived.

Tents dotted the landscape in the back of a rustic country log house and spanned as far as the crude stone wall in front of the tree line. It was a neat site and the boys were already excited about it.

"We'll spend one night camping here, since the official exodus doesn't begin until tomorrow," said Mr. Jack. "It'll give you a chance to mill around and meet the other boys. You may set up your tents wherever you choose. Do you have two or four?"

Zach answered quickly that they had only two. Cameron and Christopher would be in one, and Zach and Josiah in the other. He didn't feel to tell the group that they had discussed it with their mom before coming. She suggested that though they might like to be with their cousins, perhaps it would be better if the brothers were together at night. Jackie had said to them, "That's when that sneaky old bandit Homesickness, might try to creep in, show his pouty face, and steal some of the fun." They liked the way she had worded it, and in their chuckling were quickly able to see the wisdom behind it. It was easy to agree with reasoning like that.

They had new tents this year. Aunt Dona, who went to their home church, had given them as gifts to the travelers. She had referred to the gear as an investment in their futures. She had also bought four new sleeping bags; hardy and rugged ones like men use in the wilderness. Aunt Dona was thoughtful like that. The tents had been set up many times; however, they had never been slept in. The boys were saving them for the Exodus adventure. They had practiced setting them up and breaking them down. Pepe' had told them that they were going to wear them out before they ever used them.

"Come," Mr. Jack said to the boys, "Follow me." The boys followed as Mr. Jack walked toward the tent area. Everyone stopped what they were doing as the group approached. They looked at Mr. Jack.

"I want you to meet four boys who have come from New England," he said. "Here are Cameron and Christopher Korab, and some of you will remember Zachary Beauchene who was in the first tour group last year." Zach got a response from a group of boys gathered together in one place; chanting his name. He recognized them all from last year. Everyone clapped for the three boys who had been introduced.

A stickler for details, and extremely observant, Zachary was already taking a silent roll call to see if all the guys from last year were there. "Hey, Siah," he whispered, a bit embarrassed by the cheering squad that had greeted him. "All ten of the boys from our team last year are here. I can't wait," he said, forgetting that the crowd still had their eyes fixed on their little group.

"And," Mr. Jack continued, "I'd like to introduce the brains behind this year's adventure. You may recall he had the winning entry for the naming of last year's mascot, the feisty little mustang, Mustgofast. It would appear this young cowboy has quite an imagination. Everyone please give a rousing applause for Josiah Beauchene."

Now it was Josiah's turn to be embarrassed. Not only were the boys hooting and hollering, but the adults were all smiling and yelling as well. Suddenly he felt like a cute little boy wearing a too-big western hat. He knew he wasn't a man, but he wasn't exactly a little boy either.

He could almost hear Meme's voice saying, "Now, you be you, Josiah, and let them be them. You can only be responsible for playing your part the best way you know how." She was right. What did it matter, after all, if they thought he was just a little boy? It didn't change a thing. He would still be ten years old no matter what anyone thought. And he was going to have a wonderful time here. He had no reason to be upset or annoyed with anyone, and had absolutely nothing to prove.

"Are we the last group to come in?" asked Mr. Jack.

"Everyone but Random Mann is here, I believe," said the lady in charge of keeping such records.

"You will all set up your tents for one night here and then mill around and get acquainted. In the morning we'll assign you your groups and your leaders. In the meantime, we are one big group; a family of sorts."

Before he could continue Pete couldn't resist adding his two cents, "And, a good-looking one at that."

Everyone laughed. All the boys present from last summer's three tours all loved Pete. He had been a hit right from the start. Though he had a powerful testimony, it seemed that life had not hardened him or kicked the 'boy' out of him. He knew how to cut-up and laugh and have good clean fun. He was sensitive and seemed to relate quickly to those who were hurt for any reason, even though the reason didn't seem grand to others looking on. He could be easily touched, and the processor of his heart ran deep. Truly he was a great guy with much to offer.

His heart was tender toward the Kurdistan people. As a matter-of-fact it was he who first put his dad onto this group of forgotten ancients. Before that group ever broke the heart of Jack Harris, they had first broken the heart of his son Peter.

Mr. Jack continued, "Yes, that's true, Pete; we are a handsome lot. Now all of you must know that much thought, prayer, and expense, including your own families' and friends' contributions, have gone into this exodus experience. We want everyone to get the most out of it. So don't even think to form your own groups, boys, because it will be time wasted. That has already been taken care of. You'll hear all about it tomorrow. The only choices that were given on the forms were to those who came together. Those were asked if they would like to remain together in the same group. Otherwise, there were no other choices offered.

We'll be having a gathering of singing and just enjoying each other's company before turning in early tonight. I'm sure many of you are tired from travel. We will enjoy our last evening meal of variety tonight. We'll have grilled hot dogs, hamburgers, macaroni salad, chips, pickles, watermelon, and soda.

In the morning you'll have your last breakfast with variety before we organize to leave. Better enjoy scrambled eggs, sausage, toast, and juice, because after that it will be an exodus diet of sameness for three weeks.

We'll have an outdoor chapel service with instruction and prayer after breakfast. By then, our last leader, Mr. Random Mann, the pack animals and the chuck wagon with the supplies should be here."

Now, if you have come to know Josiah at all, the reader must already surmise that his plan is to become fast friends with at least one of the pack animals.

"If you have any questions about tonight or tomorrow morning, ask one of the leaders. They know what's going on and can answer you, I'm sure.

Now let's have some fun and make some new friends and greet some old ones. No one ever had too many friends; not real ones anyhow. If they don't introduce themselves to you; walk over and introduce yourself to them. It isn't difficult."

Immediately Josiah and Zach headed over to greet their friends from last year and to introduce Cameron and Christopher to the group.

It was like an alumni gathering; all the boys talking at once; all thrilled to see each other.

It was a happy band of boys that met that night; all one hundred, twenty of them. There was not a face that didn't wear a smile. The mood was light and the air heavy with anticipation.

Eventually, the four went back to get their tents, eager to get set up close to their 'already friends' from last year.

Both Josiah and Zach agreed that probably the group from last year would be separated this year. It was the right way to do it, they thought. That would force people to make new close friends and not form cliques and be tempted to leave others out. In fact, as the four talked about it heading for the van, they were almost certain it would be that way.

A more excited foursome would have been difficult to locate anywhere than those four that night.

They had no clue what was ahead of them, but they were already having fun and felt destined for more.

"God sure takes good care of us," said Josiah, matter-of-factly as they headed toward the group of waiting friends.

"Hey there," said someone from behind them as they were setting up their tents. The boys had been engrossed in their project, "I'm George from Los Angeles. These two boys are from the church in Mexico City. They don't speak any English but I am bilingual. Many of the folks in our church speak English and Spanish. Our pastor is able to preach in either language."

The two boys from Mexico stood by with big smiles on their faces. "They are Juanito and Roberto," George said as he pointed each out.

"Hey, I know you," said Cameron. "We saw you in some videos that Uncle Robby took from the church."

"Yah, both of you are in them," said Zach as all the boys shook hands. The four greeted Juanito and Roberto in Spanish as best they could, for they had all learned at least a little Spanish in school.

Roberto spoke and George translated. "We see you are busy setting up. We'll have plenty of time to visit in the next three weeks, so we'll let you get back to your work."

He paused as Juanito spoke through the translator, "It has been nice to meet you. I know we will be friends. We have met both your fathers and your grandparents. We feel like we know you already."

They nodded, smiled, and went back to their own tent area. The boys could hear many of that group now, speaking Spanish as they gathered around Juanito and Roberto when they returned to their tent.

"It must be nice to speak two languages equally well," said Chris to the boys when they went back to their setup work. "I would like to do that."

"It could happen," jumped in Josiah, always the optimist. "All you have to do is really want it enough and God will help you, Chris." He spoke as matter-of-factly as though Chris had asked for a cookie. "God can do anything. Look at us. We're in Colorado. Zach and I are here for the second time." He was right you know.

Chapter Nine

Where Coyotes Howl

That first night was wonderful. The temperature was a little cool there in the foothills of the Rockies, so most of the boys wore their sweatshirts. The list of clothing in the brochure included one dark colored sweatshirt without any graphics. That was simple enough, and because everyone had on blue jeans, already they looked like a single team. Even the leaders were all dressed the same. It felt good to be a part of it.

Everyone had eaten their supper on the grass near their tents. They had all been duly warned and were told that there would be no leniency; they must deposit their garbage in one of the two big containers just off the back deck. Mr. Jack told them that he wanted the yard to look as clean and litter free as it did when they had come, though he knew, of course, that there was no way it wouldn't manifest the fact that nearly one hundred, fifty people had spent a day and a night there.

The rustic log home was on the end of a long dirt drive. No other houses could be seen from here. A sturdy barn stood not far from the house. Corral fences encircled lush green pastures. The boys could see some horses off in the distance. They thought that maybe some of the animals they saw must be mules or donkeys, because they were much shorter and seemed to be stockier. Not far from the horses was a pasture of fleecy white sheep. It really was a beautiful ranch.

In the distance they could see some snow peaked mountains looming up through the fluffy clouds, no doubt pointing to the brilliant blue sky above.

After eating, the entire group joined around in a circle as Pete took his guitar and a stool to the center. His dad had asked him to play so that they could sing, or maybe just listen to the music. There was no right or wrong way to do it.

"What should I play?" Pete had asked Mr. Jack.

"You decide," Mr. Jack had answered. "It's your call, Pete. That's your unction; not mine."

Now it seems that Pete must have already given much thought and attention to this very thing, though he didn't want to presume he could play what he wanted, for the decision required little thought. He sat down and immediately began to strum.

He started with a fast-paced western song. The four boys had never heard it, though it seemed that many of the others knew it well. They liked it and were clapping their hands with the rest to the rhythm and trying to remember the chorus so they might sing with the others when it came around again. Jack and Patty both wore big smiles as they watched and listened to their son. Clearly he was in his element. It was as though his fingers were expressing that which might be difficult to put into words.

He played for about an hour. The music had slowed down as the time passed and they sang songs that allowed for a little more self-examination and reflection. Faces became more serious, though not sad, as the group meditated on the words, and in Josiah's mind, though he certainly was not the only one, the songs may as well have been prayers. It seemed the group was of one mind, and it felt great. He could almost imagine Jesus sitting in the center and actually singing with them.

Pete finished at about 8:30 with, what the boys found out later, was a song that he had written himself. The melody was beautiful; no doubt God had inspired him in the writing of it. He didn't give them the name of the song; maybe he hadn't named it.

It was not so much the words, but more the spirit behind them, as Pete sang with such feeling and humility. His voice cracked, adding to the beauty of the worship, as he struggled not to break down. Josiah had learned that one did not have to have a great voice to worship or to honor God. He had learned that the hand of the heart reaches up and plays the chords of the throat. And, that when the heart is pure, the song brings honor to God. Even as Pete sang, it seemed the glory of God had filled the outdoors, and he was sure all the others must have felt it. How could they not have?

As the four weary boys climbed into their sleeping bags they could not get some of the chorus lines out of their minds. So the weary cowboys hummed them over and over to themselves. They could almost hear the soft strumming of the guitar and Pete's voice as they rehearsed some of the words replaying like the most beautiful lullaby.

And, how can I thank You, LORD
For calling me out of Egypt
Help me to appreciate
The ransom that you paid...

Off in the distance the coyotes howled, as the four boys drifted off to sleep to the echo of Pete's music, born, no doubt, from his own experience.

Chapter Ten

Everybody Present and Accounted For

In spite of the fact that they had been tired the night before, the four boys rose early the next morning. Not too many of the others were milling around. Of course it was two hours later at home, so to them it didn't seem early at all.

The woman of the house, along with her husband, was busy preparing to cook breakfast on the back deck. The morning fog was over the mountains and the air was a bit chilly, but it promised to be a beautiful day.

"Man, did I sleep," said Cameron. "How about you guys?"

"Like a baby," answered Chris.

"I didn't realize how tired I was," added Zach, to which Josiah was quick to agree.

Already into their day clothes, they were ready to pull down and roll up their tents, but thought they had better wait for the word to go ahead.

Josiah was hoping the day would start early. Even at home, they were all up early and raring to get on with the things that awaited them in the new day. So much more they did not want to waste any of their precious time out here. "I wonder when Mr. Jack and the rest will get up?" he said to the others.

Just then he spotted Mr. Jack with his wife coming out of the house onto the back deck, holding coffee cups. "Hey, gang," he greeted. "I figured I'd find you up when I came out. It's almost six o'clock. We're going to sound the wake-up call in a few minutes."

The boys were pleased to see that Pete was up as he was coming from the section where Roberto and Juanito had camped for the night. Juanito was walking beside him with a shofar. As they approached the back deck, Juanito stopped and turned when he had passed the area where the tents were. Pete spoke something to him and he raised the shofar, and put it to his lips. The clearest, most beautiful sound seemed to halt even the singing birds, as Juanito blew three short and one long blast from the instrument, as it resonated through the whole campsite. He repeated that series three times in succession before he turned and walked with Pete to greet the boys.

"Buenos Dias," smiled and greeted all the boys before he had a chance to greet them. How surprised they were when Juanito smiled and answered them, halting a little to pronounce the words, "Good morning."

Everyone laughed, as, after that, they were clearly at a loss for words. Boys and their leaders popped their heads out of tents everywhere as the camp became alive with activity.

Less than forty-five minutes later they were all sitting to breakfast, enjoying the last of the bounty of variety, even as they were told they should by Mr. Jack last night.

The four boys had been the first to finish their eating, as they had been the first served. It seems the cooks had insisted on it.

"Can we roll up our tents now, Mr. Jack?" asked Josiah, who found it very hard to wait.

"Sure," he said. "That's a good idea. "If the rest see you doing it, they'll more than likely follow suit as soon as they're done eating."

Each of the boys made a tight roll of his tent, sleeping bag, and the thin travel pillows they had taken with them. They would miss their thicker pillows from back home, but they weren't allowed on this trip. They had put a roll of clothes under their sleeping bags to lift their heads off the ground, and that had worked just fine. Meme' would have been proud of them if she could see them now. She would have said, as she was so fond of quoting, "You boys know that necessity is the mother of invention." The four had really come to understand that and that it was true.

Just as they were finishing the tent rolls, off in the distance they could see what looked like trail riders coming down the dirt drive. A small wagon, probably the chuck wagon, they guessed, was pulled by two mules or donkeys, they weren't sure which. Tied to the back of the wagon was a string of other animals, following in single file. Josiah was thrilled as he felt that in that group of animals there was at least one good friend to be made. Of that he was certain. After all, he thought optimistically, they really didn't look that different from horses.

The man driving the wagon turned out to be none other than Mr. Random Mann. He wore a smile that seemed to involve his whole face as he nodded in greeting to the group. Jumping down from his seat he quickly approached Mr. Jack and Mrs. Patty. "I'm Random Mann," he said. "I know your faces already from the church. I'm happy to finally meet you and I thank you for allowing me to come along as an extra."

Mr. Jack, embracing the man in greeting, smiled and spoke genuinely. "There's no such thing as extras around here, my friend. We're probably happier to have you along than you are to come. My son Pete has spoken much and often about you. Patty and I feel as though we already know you."

"Thank you," returned Random, "and you all please call me Randy. All my friends do."

Josiah and Zach looked at each other and smiled. On the trip last year, one of the men who had traveled with them from the ranch was named Randy. Both boys; in fact, all the boys, had liked him very much.

"Speaking of Randy," said Mr. Jack. "Our old friend Randy from last summer's trip wanted me to deliver a message to you, Josiah. Gee, I almost forgot," he said, smiling. "Now where did I put it?"

"Patty," he said to his wife who was talking with one of the other ladies. "Do you know where I left Randy's message for Josiah?"

"My goodness, Jack Harris," she answered as though scolding him. "You need me and there's just no doubt about it. You'd forget your head if it wasn't attached."

"Oops, I must have left it in the van," he said as Patty walked back toward the barn where the vehicles were parked. "She'll find it," he added.

In the meantime they all walked toward the wagon and the animals with Randy. The chuck wagon looked like a small Conestoga. The canvas enclosed its contents on all four sides, so the boys couldn't even get a look at the food and whatever else was packed in there. Josiah didn't know about the rest, but he was sure curious to see inside, pretty much the way he was about everything. That was just his nature, you understand.

"Are these mules or donkeys?" he asked of nobody in particular. "They look a little like a horse."

"Well," answered Randy, as all the boys listened. "These animals are mules. And you are right, Josiah. They have a strong resemblance to the horse because one of their parents is a horse, and the other is a donkey."

"Oh, so that's it," one of the boys added from the back. "I always wondered about that myself."

Josiah busied himself with petting one of the two in the front of the wagon. He was lost already in attempting to make a friend of the animal so much so that he noticed nothing going on around him. For all he knew it was simply he and the mule.

He was snapped from his dream world when Mr. Jack spoke to him. "Oh, Josiah, Patty found the message, just as I knew she would. Here it is."

Josiah turned to receive it. He stared in disbelief and seemed unable to make his feet move. "Mustgofast!" he shouted as the horse stood only three or four feet from him; Mrs. Patty holding the bridle.

Mustgofast immediately closed the distance between them; Josiah still unable to budge. The horse put his face down against Josiah's chest as he 'talked' softly to 'his boy,' giving him a little nudge. Unable to stop them, the tears streamed down Josiah's face, close now against the face of the mustang, so familiar and dear to his heart. The softness of the side of Mustgofast's face and even the smell made him want to cry all the more.

No one said a word until finally Mr. Jack cleared his throat. "The ranch brought him over a few days ago. They said they couldn't see how you two could be so close and not be able to visit each other. It was actually their idea to loan him out as the mascot for our Stopping Places exodus, that is, as long as you're up to it, because he will be under your care. You have to understand that you'll have to walk with the others, because this isn't a horseback trail ride. So, what do you think?"

Josiah, who was still unable to talk, nodded his head. As though that needed interpretation, Zachary, who was also choked up, jumped in to help his brother. "He says that he would like that," he answered simply. "And I think the rest of us would too."

A cheer went up from the crowd, but Josiah barely heard it as they seemed so far off in the distance. Clearly, now everyone was present and accounted for.

Everyone was happy, but no one was happier than Josiah. As far as he was concerned, if this was for him the greatest and only high point of the trip out west, then already it was enough and he had much to be thankful for.

Chapter Eleven

The Inheritance

"It had been a long journey," Mr. Jack began, almost sadly as everyone was seated in the grass that morning. His mysterious tone already captivating his audience, he continued, "But God was calling His people, Israel, home. They had lived amongst the Egyptians and their false gods for four hundred and thirty years. They had forgotten their God and the promises that he had given to their father Abraham.

He had their attention now, as for many years they had been little more than slaves in the land of Egypt. Were that not enough, it had been brought to the attention of the Pharaoh, that even under these circumstances their population was increasing with strong, healthy babies. The Egyptians feared a takeover.

The favor of the Pharaoh who was the singular man over Joseph, the son of Jacob, had vanished long ago. Joseph had reminded the people that one day they would return to their own land; that land that had been promised by God to Abraham, Isaac, and Jacob, and to their descendants. 'When you do return,' he commissioned even as he was dying, 'take my bones with you and bury them in that land; the land of my fathers.'

God allowed even more tribulation to come upon the Israelites so that they might remember to call to Him. When the Egyptians then, began to kill all the male babies, throwing them into the Nile River, they cried out to God. At about that time a baby boy was born, and hidden in a basket which had been fashioned by his own parents, that he might have hope of being spared the fate of the Israelite babies. Into the very same river those babies had been thrown, these loving parents placed their beautiful three-month old son. His sister Miriam watched from a distance what might happen to her baby brother as he floated up the Nile River, for the Nile flows north, you see. She watched as the Pharaoh's daughter who was going to go into the water sent her handmaiden to fetch the basket. She took note to how beautiful this baby was, and because the baby wept, she had compassion on him and took him as her own. She knew he must be a Hebrew baby, but it was love at first sight."

Mr. Jack continued to hold everyone's attention as he told the story in a way that few can tell. (Now if the reader has ever heard Mr. Jack relate a story, you recognize that there is no exaggeration here.) The boys, actually adults too, were spellbound, even though, no doubt, all of them had heard the story before. But, somehow, in this particular setting, amongst this particular group, as is so much God's way, the words took on a different meaning.

"And so," Mr. Jack continued, "the Pharaoh's daughter took the baby to be her own, and called him Moses, that means 'drawn from the water'.

Off in the distance little Miriam watched what would happen to her baby brother. When the Pharaoh's daughter lifted him up tenderly from the basket the little girl ran to her, asking if she would like Miriam to run and get a Hebrew woman to feed and care for the child. No doubt the Pharaoh's daughter thought this would be best as so many of the Hebrew women had lost their baby boys, and continued to, in the massacre. She may have felt these would make the best caretakers after losing their own sons. And so, you see, Moses' own mother took him to her home and cared for her son and was paid to do it by the Pharaoh's daughter.

When the baby was old enough his mother took him back to the palace where he was raised as royalty.

Imagine," Mr. Jack paused here, "I mean, just imagine if the Pharaoh could have had a sneak peak of what the future held for Egypt through this insignificant looking baby boy who would become a deliverer of the people of God?

When he was forty, Moses killed one of the Pharaoh's men for abusing a Hebrew slave. He buried him in the sand. But the next day two of the Hebrew men were fighting and Moses asked his brethren who was in the wrong, why he beat upon the other.

The Israelite man turned to him and asked him who had made him prince and judge over them and whether he intended to kill them as he had killed the Egyptian the previous day.

Moses became fearful that he would be found out by the Pharaoh for having killed an Egyptian, and, rightfully so, for when the Pharaoh found out, he was looking to kill Moses. Moses fled a great distance away where he felt the Pharaoh would not pursue him. He went to the land of Midian which is on the eastern coast of the Red Sea, not far from Mt. Sinai.

There Moses married and lived for forty more years. I'm sure you all know the story of the burning bush. One day God spoke to Moses about hearing the cries of His people, Israel, from the land of Egypt. They were now ready to be delivered, as they had had enough Egyptian tyranny and they remembered their God."

Mr. Jack became rather solemn as he reflected aloud, almost as though he were talking to himself. Like the song that his son Pete had sung that first night, it gave his message so much more meaning.

"Isn't it remarkable," he said, "how much it takes sometimes for God to get our attention? We can accept so much of ourselves and our situations that we don't even look for God to change or help us. We just keep traveling through that same rut, maybe just because we are used to it and, really, it is little more than an endless grave?

Anyway," he continued, snapping himself back to the crowd he was standing before, "God had tried for many years to get the attention of Israel, but had to resort to more difficult measures. You may wonder why He even cares that much. I mean, why not scrap the whole project and start over? Or just call it a fruitless plan, and forget about mankind who had become so evil and destroy them all."

Some of the crowd actually chuckled when he said that so matter-of-factly. It was that real down-to-earth approach that endeared Mr. Jack to his listeners to begin with.

"Certainly, God could have done something else with His time. I mean, He's God!

But He loved His people too much to leave them alone. He simply could not let go of His greatest creation without expressing even more love; not tolerance for their sin, but love for these weak human vessels. After all, He had a great inheritance for them.

Besides, He had made a promise to Abraham, and then to Isaac, and his son Jacob. He was not a man that He could lie and not keep His promises. What He said He would do, He would do. My thought is," and here Mr. Jack laughed, "I mean, who would know anyway? It isn't like God has to answer to somebody else? But the fact is that God swears by Himself, and He is truth. He has told us that He would do and perform exactly what He said He would. Even as He told Noah, for example, that He promised never again to destroy the earth by flooding it. We can be sure that when this world comes to an end, it will not be a flood that does it. That was a sort of water baptism; the next will be a baptism of fire.

One day Moses, who was now married, was keeping the sheep of his father-in-law, on the back side of the desert near Mt. Horeb. No doubt, he was minding his own business there. Mt. Horeb is the Mountain of God, part of the Mt. Sinai chain. He saw a bush that appeared to be burning, but yet was not destroyed. He said, 'I must turn aside and go see this great sight', and so he did.

The Angel of the LORD spoke from the bush, calling Moses forth and telling him to remove his sandals, for he was on holy ground. The One in the bush was none other than the LORD Himself.

He told Moses that He had heard the cry of the people and had come down to deliver them out of Egypt and into the land that was a good and a large land that flowed with milk and honey.

He wanted them to come into their inheritance; that which God had promised their forefathers, and it was time. He would send Moses to Egypt now that the Pharaoh was dead and would no longer pursue him, and the LORD would use him as His right arm of deliverance for the Israelite people.

In this story," he continued, after a brief pause, "Egypt represents the world that doesn't know Christ and the Promised Land represents that inheritance God has for us. It is very important to God, because it has cost Him much and His investment is great. Because of His love for us, He wants us to know peace, and joy, and a type of prosperity in this life that all the money in the world cannot buy.

Like the Israelites, many of us live in the wilderness and have not ever reached the Promised Land. And, many even die in the wilderness. That is not to say that we don't know the LORD, and many will go on to spend eternity with Him. But, rather, that is to say that some never enjoy the life that has been purchased for them at great price, because they have never gotten their hands on their inheritance and enjoyed the land of milk and honey.

Here is where we come in. We want to do at least two things during this trip. In this Stopping Places exodus, we want to appreciate what the LORD has done by calling us out of Egypt. No one is born knowing the LORD. We make a conscious decision to serve Him and to walk away from Egypt, that is, the things the world holds dear, and into our great heritage bought for us on the cross. But there are battles to be fought as we head for that land of milk and honey.

We will see, by comparison, I hope, what the Israelites, that is, the Hebrews, went through that we might find the parallel in our own lives. We hope to witness, first hand, the type of life that many of the Kurdistan people still live today, though, for us, it is a choice, while they have none.

And now, back to our friend Moses. God used Moses to call down nine plagues against the people and the land of Egypt. God protected the Hebrew people to show them His love and His power and His intention to deliver them from the hand of the Pharaoh and the power of Egypt. The Pharaoh would not let the people go until finally God visited them with the tenth plague; the death of the firstborn in every Egyptian home. Again He spared the Israelites, as they put blood on their doorposts that the angel of death might supernaturally pass over them. With this the Pharaoh finally let, no, forced the Israelites to leave.

This is the place where we will pick up the story.

We have just left Egypt and are on our way to the Promised Land. We are after our inheritance; not because we've earned it, but because He has left it to us. Shame on us if we don't consider it worth going after, since He felt it worth dying for. It is meant for us in this life, on this side of heaven, that those from Egypt will know that our God is real and He still lives and moves amongst His people. The LORD has told us that the people fall by the wayside because they don't even realize what is available to them. So, are we ready boys?"

Dramatically the entire group stood to their feet and gave a rousing cheer as though they might have been staging a grand pep rally.

"The time was so notable to the LORD," Mr. Jack went on," that He told the people that from then on their calendar would change to make the time of the Passover a time of new beginnings. He instructed them this day would be celebrated as the beginning of each Jewish New

Year. It was called Abib and later changed to Nisan. It coincides with our mid-March to mid-April."

As Mr. Jack was finishing, Random Mann walked out toward the chuck wagon, took out two canvas signs, and tied one to either side of the Conestoga cover.

They said simply:

STOPPING PLACES
PROMISED LAND or BUST

Again, the crowd cheered.

Chapter Twelve

A Labor of Love

"Now we are going to break up to travel in our respective tribes," Mr. Jack continued. "We will first call out the names of the leaders; all twelve sets of them; each to lead one tribe according to the names of the tribes of Israel. This won't take long. Listen carefully. Even as the people of Israel did not just all run out of Egypt, we too must have a plan to eliminate chaos, right? We need plans, planners, and organization in our lives.

As we travel, each boy will stay with his tribe. Between the last meal of the day and bedtime, you may join each other as you wish. Of course, we will all travel together anyway. None of us will be too far apart. After we separate the twelve sets of leaders, each boy will hear his name called out to a particular tribe. You will gather with your leaders. Pete will call out your names, as he has done a great deal of work organizing this whole part of the exodus. While he may not know you personally, he is very familiar with your names."

Immediately Pete took the front and began to separate the leaders. It didn't take long. Already the group seemed to catch the spirit of organization. He began with the leaders' names, and then proceeded to call out the ten boys who would be part of that team. He began with Reuben, and continued with Simeon, Judah, Issachar, Zebulun, Benjamin, Dan, Naphtali, Gad, Asher, and Joseph. Last of all he called out the tribe of Levi. Moses had been a Levite and, of course, had led the Exodus. Being as Mr. Jack would hold that position, he, Mrs. Patty, and Pete would be as one leader and Random Mann the other of the tribe of Levi. The leaders had been told, even before they arrived, which tribe they would represent so the process went rapidly. In fifteen minutes each boy was in his respective group.

Only one of the boys from last year's team was in the tribe of the Levites. Zach and Siah were not surprised that it was Brian, the boy who they referred to as the 'Cashite'. He played most of Johnny Cash's songs on his guitar; a favorite of Mr. Jack. They knew that Pete had purposed to put him in the same tribe so they could play together. And, there was no doubt in their minds that he must have his guitar along with him. "Of course," whispered Zach to the boys, "that's really the way it should be. Remember Meme' saying that Asaph and the musicians were from the tribe of Levi?"

Juanito and Roberto were also part of their group along with two boys who could translate for them. The other Spanish speaking boys were scattered throughout the other tribes. Only one of the others could not speak English. It seemed right and fitting that Juan and Roberto should be with them as Levites, as Juanito would be playing his shofar.

"Randy tells me that he has made a little something for each of us, which is why he couldn't join us yesterday. He wasn't quite done with his project," said Mr. Jack as soon as everyone was in his respective tribe. "To tell you the truth, I have no idea what it is he has done, but I can barely wait to see it." As he spoke, Randy went back to the chuck wagon and came back with a hand-carved staff for Mr. Jack. Shyly he presented it to him in front of the crowd without a great deal of ceremony.

"I made you this that you could carry it as a remembrance of not only this trip, but of what the LORD has already done in your life. It has on it your family name, your tribe, and today's date. You may write on it when you wish to: the things God has done, the things He is doing, and His promises for the future. After all, the exodus was about the Promised Land."

Mr. Jack was overwhelmed. It was beautiful. It had, no doubt, been taken from a live tree. Somehow, even that was symbolic. It fit perfectly in his hand. The staff was not perfectly straight, but had a bit of a crook in it about a third of the way down. Somehow, that added to its beauty.

The clearest Biblical picture flashed in his mind of Moses with his staff. Mr. Jack choked up at the symbolism and the thought that must have motivated the crafting of this staff. "I don't really know what to say," his voice sounding raspy even to himself. "Randy, this is tremendous. You must have worked so hard on it. I can't tell you how I appreciate your thoughtfulness."

Randy smiled, pleased by Jack's reaction. "I'll be right back," he said. He asked Pete to go with him as he walked to the little wagon. Together they hauled armfuls of staffs: one for each husband and wife and one for each of the boys. Everyone was overwhelmed as Pete called out the name of the tribe and then the boy's name.

"How did you have time to do all this?" asked Mr. Jack.

"Well, as soon as I knew I was coming, I got to work. Most of them I made by myself, but toward the end, as the time drew near, I asked some of the men in the church to give me a hand. They were happy to help and we enjoyed the making of them, but, even more, the time together. It was good to have my house full of men again. I haven't done much of that since my wife Sylvia died. It was like a good medicine. And, check this out; they even made one for me."

No one would have been convinced that this man had been depressed. His face already reflected the joy that comes with knowing the LORD.

"I see," said Mr. Jack when the handing of the staffs was completed, "that, already the LORD is working. Isn't it wonderful?"

Everyone gave a loud cheer and applauded Randy.

"Notice how unique every rod is," Mr. Jack continued. "Even that means so much to me." He wasn't alone in his thinking. There was not a person there who didn't appreciate the fullness of it; right down to the youngest recipient. It was a labor of love. And, it was very possible that already, if all the rods were laid down with the names toward the ground, each person could pick out his own rod.

"These are going to be great for walking," said Cameron, "and for snakes. Boy, are they neat." And, they were.

Chapter Thirteen

The Long Walk Home

Pete told Josiah that he could go to the barn to get Mustgofast. He didn't need to be told twice. Randy went with him while Pete organized the order of packing the mules and carrying the supplies.

There were twenty-four mules, besides those pulling the cart. Each team would have to make do with two mules. That should pose no problem, as each person had been allowed three complete sets of clothing for the daytime, and two for the nighttime; two sweatshirts, a pair of shorts, and a vinyl, light rain jacket, placed in a small duffle bag along with their toiletries, as well as a short clothesline, some clothespins and a bar of laundry soap. Of course, one of the three sets of clothing they wore. The boys in each group would alternate the responsibility of caring for the two mules; leading them by their reins, brushing them down each night, and seeing that they were tied where they would have food, water, and safety. Besides that there were the tents, which were light and small. The mules were more than able to carry their load with little effort, and, who knows, perhaps would even enjoy the exodus themselves.

Each person had a small backpack which he would carry. In it were his Bible, a notepad, two pens, a small flashlight, bug spray, a whistle (in case he somehow needed help), and a canteen. He could also carry a mouth harp or harmonica if he chose. There were no electronics, except for a special solar battery field cell phone for use by Mr. Jack and Random Mann, in case of emergencies, and cameras, of course. Randy, after all, was in charge of the animals and the supplies, while, of course, Mr. Jack was responsible for the people. All the other supplies were in the small Conestoga wagon.

As soon as Pete returned with Josiah leading Mustgofast, Randy asked if he and Pete could take turns driving the wagon. He said that it had been a long while since he had gone out and just walked. For him and Sylvia that had been a great pastime and he looked forward to getting back into it. Pete quickly agreed and asked who would take the first day. Randy simply smiled, holding his staff in front of him; backpack fastened securely over his shoulders, and with that, Pete tossed his pack and staff up onto the seat. He didn't need an interpreter to understand Randy's response.

Everyone had his backpack on, his staff in hand, and was ready to go.

"Before we begin to walk," said Mr. Jack, "I have a few things to say, and then, of course, we will pray. Even as I told you earlier, let me say some of this again to set the scenario for the day. It is a new day in Egypt. Our people have been here for four hundred, thirty years; actually, to the day. How precise is that? Now, God is calling us home. His judgment has just passed over us; every one of us, for no good reason except that somewhere in the back of our minds, we remembered Him and He has heard our cry, even, as it is obvious, someone in Kurdistan is crying out for help, and to understand what is going on in their lives. If you listen carefully you will hear and respond to their cry, for God has given to the faithful Christian, excellent hearing.

In a way, you see, Egypt was a wilderness of sorts, though we did not recognize it, and we have been there for over ten generations. It was not meant to be our permanent residence here on earth. We have been slack in our duties and the commitment of our fathers, Abraham, Isaac, and Jacob, to seek out the promises of God, but after much hardship, the LORD has gotten our attention. Most of us have been following the Egyptian gods and become very familiar with their ways.

Pharaoh did not want to let us go, but God has insisted, and, finally, after the tenth plague, the death of the firstborn, Pharaoh has agreed that we *must* leave. The Egyptians, preoccupied with death in every home, have given us much wealth, even as God said they would. All of Egypt is in mourning, and, as far as they were concerned, we couldn't leave quickly enough.

In the New Testament, *Egypt* represents the world without Christ. Sometimes it is hard to walk away from the things of the world, for they are very familiar, but it is the plan of God that we do just that. The Father has told us that He has provision for us, a Promised Land of our own, bought and paid for by the blood of His only Begotten Son, Jesus. It is far greater than anything the world has to offer.

This trek, **Stopping Places**, represents not only those hurtles, trials, and battles that the Israelites experienced, but those that are common to us today. They are relevant in the life of every Christian, and have to do with the provision of God for His children; after all, He is a good Father.

Remember as we walk through the wilderness, those Kurdistan people in Iraq, as you experience in part the lives they are forced to lead.

Even at this, of course, we have it far better than they, as far as variety of provision and homes and loved ones waiting for us when we leave this place. But, they live in a good land, full of resources, and the same Father Who provides for us, is looking to become their Provider. His arm is not short.

Right now, we have a problem. If you are familiar with the book of Exodus, you know what it is. We won't try to pretend we don't know the story. We know that Pharaoh, though he thought he had, has not had enough yet. God Himself had hardened this man's heart so that he would continue to pursue the Hebrew people.

Many have asked why God would do such a thing. The reading of it may even make God seem cruel. God, you see, has two sides: judgment and mercy. It is for us to decide which side of Him we wish to bring out. His desire is to show us mercy, but when we don't receive it, He has a very terrible side as well, especially in defense of His Own people, and, the final say will always belong to Him. I, for one, wish to stay on His 'good' side; though, for sure He has no bad side.

The Bible tells us that God would bless those who bless Israel and curse those who curse them. He does not lie. It may seem that He takes His time, and, in effect this is true; everything is in His time.

The Egyptians had oppressed and used the Israelites; even killing their baby boys. God saw that as no small thing, even as He sees it as no small thing today. Children, you see, are a gift from God. He has said that Israel was the apple of His eye. Of course, after Christ went to the cross, the bond became even stronger between the Father and those who follow Him, as He has invested the best that heaven had, His Own dear Son, in this relationship. So, neither is that any small thing. He is looking to provide for and bless those who respond to His Own sacrifice and the sacrifice of His son, Jesus."

A rousing "Amen" resounded from the group, as though they were all of one voice. Mrs. Patty thought about how incredible their response was, and was thrilled by it. Something in her had wanted to scream a heartier response; so much was she in agreement with her husband.

Already she was glad that Jack had responded to Josiah's email the way he had. She knew that much would be gleaned from these three weeks in the wilderness and that, if they were willing, everyone would be better for the time, money, and effort spent.

She knew that they must keep their eyes opened as, for certain, the enemy was already angry about this gathering. But, she thought, they would fight the good fight and stay sober and vigilant. She chuckled to herself as she thought that she sounded like she might be reading a text or two from the Bible. She liked it when that happened.

"And so," Mr. Jack continued, "we are on our way. We don't realize it yet, but the Pharaoh shall come after us. Let us pray, then, and proceed to the first of the stopping places."

With that, each tribe joined hands and together prayed in agreement with Jack Harris as he held his wife Patty's hand on one side and Josiah's on the other. It was a very happy, expectant, though serious group that prayed that day. There was not a heart that had not been touched by Mr. Jack's introduction. They could almost taste the adventure ahead of them, and the danger waiting to pursue from behind. The air was electric with anticipation. ""Sons of Jacob; the *supplanters,*" said Mr. Jack forcefully, "let us begin our long walk home."

Chapter Fourteen

Tent Pegs

As soon as they began their walk Josiah realized that it wouldn't be necessary to hold Mustgofast's reins constantly and lead him. The horse, as though they had not been away from each other at all, had no desire it seemed, to move away from his boy. He followed close behind Josiah, nuzzling him every now and then for a little attention. Josiah was at his peak. He couldn't be any more contented if he had been sitting on his mustang's back and they were racing through the green grasses of an open meadow. This kind of companionship was hard to come by and mustn't be reduced to a horseback ride.

Every once in a while the boys in his group asked Josiah's permission to pet the mustang's back, or stroke his mane. Of course, Josiah quickly agreed to grant their request. Even to him it felt the right thing that they should ask him. Had he not been told, after all, that Mustgofast was entirely his responsibility for the next three weeks?

In every group happy chatter could be heard. It was a beautifully clear day with white wispy clouds streaking the ever-so-blue sky. It was as though God Himself had painted a magnificent mural for their beginning day to mark the promise of the future and to encourage perseverance. Everyone was happy; though possibly no one happier than Josiah. (His closest rival may have been Random Mann, though I don't rightly know him that well at this point to make the call.)

The groups hung closely together as they headed across the flat plane toward the mountains off in the distance. The grass was green and grasshoppers and more insects than they could focus on hopped or flew from one delicacy to another in this grand buffet of variety. It seemed as though even they were celebrating the day, or, at least the smorgasbord laid out for them.

They walked for about an hour when Mr. Jack called a ten-minute halt to enjoy some water from their canteens, filled at the cabin before they left, and a single piece of beef jerky for anyone who wanted it.

"Remember," Mr. Jack began, and everyone quieted as they sat on the grass sipping from their canteens and chewing their beef jerky, "we have just left Rameses, in the land of Goshen. There were 600,000 men between twenty and forty years old, besides women and children. They had all their flocks and cattle. They had the gold, silver, jewelry, and rich clothing that had been given to them by the Egyptians. God, you see, had plans for that finery. They had been little more than slaves and had little to claim as their own but their families and livestock. They did not feel they had to run, for the Pharaoh had forced them to leave in the middle of the night, lest *all* of Egypt should die. We have with us the unleavened dough and our kneading boards, for we were warned by the LORD through Moses that when we left, we must leave in a hurry. Imagine if you will that we are them. We, of course, would not be eating jerky.

We have been told by Moses and his brother Aaron that God has spoken and that for the next seven days we must celebrate the LORD'S great Passover and the blood of the lamb that had halted God's judgment just outside our doors. Of course today the New Testament Lamb, Jesus Christ, does the same only we celebrate that every day. It is not meant to be a once-a-year remembrance, but an everyday occurrence in our lives.

The people, that is, *us*, were happy to obey what Moses had told them they must do, for they were ecstatic about their deliverance from bondage. The Bible says it so beautifully. I love this portion of text.

And you shall observe this thing for an ordinance to you and to your sons forever.

And it shall come to pass, when you have come to the land which the LORD will give you, according as he has promised, that you shall keep this service.

And it shall come to pass, when your children shall say unto you, "What mean ye by this service?"

That you shall say, "It is the sacrifice of the LORD'S passover, who passed over the houses of the children of Israel in Egypt, when he smote the Egyptians, and delivered our houses." And the people bowed the head and worshipped.

Exodus 12: 24-27

Isn't that beautiful?

It was midnight when the LORD visited every home in Egypt with death. We left shortly after that while it was still dark. I will say, even as Moses did, 'Remember this day, in which ye came out from Egypt, out of the house of bondage; for by strength of hand the LORD brought you out from this place.' "

Again, everyone was wrapped up in the words that Mr. Jack shared with them. He himself was caught up in the telling of the story which had already come alive in this group.

"This is why the orthodox Jew today offers the firstborn male of every clean animal as a sacrifice to the LORD; because the LORD required the firstborn male in every Egyptian home. He wanted them to remember what He had done because of His love for them.

Keep in mind as we walk through the wilderness, that each stopping place represents a critical point in our lives. Decision is the key factor. We may go the way of our enemy Satan, the way of the flesh, which is also our enemy, or God's way. Those are always the three choices we are given. When we make a wrong choice, we miss out on a promise, or the timing of one, that our Father means for us to walk toward or hold in our hands. It is that simple.

Now, notice that we have been traveling toward the south. That is the same direction that Pete has mapped out for us. He has gone to a great deal of trouble to imitate, as closely as he could, the direction of the travel of the Israelites. Though we couldn't do it perfectly, we have tried to stick to the script as best we could in most areas.

The LORD, you see, did not take the Israelites by the shortest route or more direct path. They would have had to pass through the land of the Philistines, a very warring people, who would, no doubt, have made war against the Hebrew people. For over ten generations the

Israelites had lived as a peaceful people. They did what was expected of them. They neither went to war, nor did they train their children to war. They knew little of it and had absolutely no experience in it. Had the Philistines come against them, God felt they would be tempted to turn back to the relative safety of Egypt.

It is so important that we walk under the direction of God. If we do not, we may encounter something more than we are able to handle. So many wonder where God was in their time of trial, but the truth is that they were not where they should have been and are suffering the consequences of either ignorance or rebellion. It is so common to 'flesh-out' and go where our own flesh wants to take us. Comments such as 'of course the shorter way is best' have gotten many unsuspecting Christians into a heap of trouble bigger than themselves."

About an hour after they had started walking again, they stopped for a late lunch. It was after one o'clock and it seemed a good place to stop with a shaded area to rest beneath. Randy went to the wagon and took out some flatbread. He called the tribes forward, one at a time, to pick up a round, nine-inch bread, and a piece of jerky. "Go easy on your water," he said, "because we won't be filling the canteens any time soon. We must make it last until we can fill them tonight. Remember, the Israelites didn't know where the next running water was. We want somewhat of an authentic feel behind this thing. Or, at least, that is my understanding. Don't eat your food too quickly. Chew it carefully, allow your mouth to taste it, then your body will digest it correctly. Remember too, the Israelites had no idea how long they would be traveling. It was a relatively short distance between Rameses in the land of Goshen and Canaan. The trip shouldn't take long. Of course there were many people, herds of animals, elderly, and very young, to deal with, besides the fact that they didn't know what lay ahead for them. They knew better than to be careless with what they had."

Everyone was surprised by such a lengthy speech from the one who had been so quiet to this point. It was clear he felt a responsibility, in particular with food and provisions, where the group was concerned.

As they took their time eating, they drank in the grandeur of the scenery. A lone eagle soared high above, no doubt riding the currents rising from the far-off mountains. Josiah thought of how much fun it looked to be as the majestic bird seemingly without effort, cruised the unmarked highways of the skies. He knew the eagle didn't miss much. He had extremely sharp eyes and could spot even a very small animal far beneath him, and drop to the ground quickly and with precision. No doubt the eagle was watching them even now. "I wonder what he must be thinking," Josiah thought. Siah enjoyed science and was always listening and observing the details of nature even when he wasn't in school. It was just in him to do it.

In a short time they were back on their feet, continuing toward the first stopping place. "The wilderness that the LORD has chosen for us is the Wilderness of the Red Sea," said Mr. Jack, as they were walking. "Over the years the exact location of some of the Biblical names of the places has either been changed or lost, but we will waste no time on arguing exact routes, for that would be pointless and serve no good purpose but controversy. That is not the point of this trip. Let us leave that to the Pharisees.

A conservative estimate would be that there were at least between two and three million Israelites in all; maybe more. The Bible tells us that they formed an orderly rank. A normal day's journey for the Jew was about ten miles. They could probably not have traveled that distance as there were so many, but their journey began not long after midnight. Estimates range from about ten to twenty-five miles between Rameses and Succoth, the first stopping place. There is no reason to believe they would have stopped before they reached this place, this of course being their first day of travel, their release from bondage, and their first adrenaline surge of liberty, all good motivators to press on.

There is no doubt that later they had slowed their course, but the Bible clearly states that there were times that they traveled by night and day."

"Succoth!" repeated Josiah, "Now I remember the name of one of the places, Zach."

Down the knoll on the edge of the prairie stood a sign that was handwritten **Succoth**. Everyone was excited when Josiah called it out. Even Mustgofast came up beside him now, sensing, or so it seemed, his master's excitement.

All four of the boys wanted to run toward the place but held back if only for the sake of not looking childish. "Boy," said Mr. Jack, "doesn't seeing that just make you wanna' run. If I was just a little younger, I'd be the first one there."

He grinned at Josiah, and it appeared that had they been racing, Josiah might have been able to beat Mustgofast to the spot where the sign stood; a stampede of boys following close behind the two.

A minute later Mr. Jack arrived with the rest of the troops. "Now boys," he said, trying to muster up some disappointment by their outburst of energy, "what am I going to do with you? You've broken rank!"

Everyone laughed as Mr. Jack could not keep a straight face. There in a zipped plastic bag stapled behind the sign were first-day journeyman's papers for all who made it to this important place. Pete quickly had Roberto hand one out to each person. Each was the size of an index card and meant as a memento of the first night in the wilderness.

"The name *Succoth*" Mr. Jack began, "literally means tent or tabernacle. It was the place where Israel would spend their first night free of Egyptian bondage and set up their tents or tabernacles.

Now, for us today it has a different significance. That is what we are looking for. What does that have to do with us?

The LORD has just told us to leave Egypt, that is, to come away from the ways of the world and to follow His ways. We have voluntary walked away. From the first that we decide and act upon it, we become His tent or tabernacle.

Let us assume then, that we have all given our lives to Him, therefore, we are headed for heaven one day when this life is done, but walking toward the promises of God while we still live in these tabernacles, or tents.

Paul said, [1]'For we know that if our earthly house of this tabernacle were dissolved, we have a building of God, a house not made with hands, eternal in the heavens.' These tents or tabernacles are to be set down with tent pegs that are temporary, for we are on a journey with the LORD. When He says, 'Pull the tent pegs,' that is what we must do. Remember, this is not our home.

Peter said, [2]'I think it meet, as long as I am in this tabernacle, to stir you up by putting you in remembrance; knowing that shortly I must put off this my tabernacle, even as our Lord Jesus Christ has shown me.'

We are not nervous. We have just experienced the greatest demonstration of God's deliverance; the greatest miracle; our own salvation ~ a personal Passover. We are tired, but there is a feeling of expectancy, excitement, and adventure. We don't know what to expect, but we know in Whom we have put our trust. All is well."

---

[1] 2 Cor. 5: 1 KJV
[2] 2 Peter 1: 13-14 KJV

Together they began to set up their tents under the inspiration of the words of Mr. Jack and the mood that came with it. Pete took out his guitar and began to play a well-known song and as they worked they all sang. Those who did not know the song picked it up quickly. It was lively and powerful and it had to do with knowing Who it is we believe in.

Josiah thought he caught Randy crying a little, and wasn't exactly sure why, for the song was so upbeat. He knew though, that everything didn't hit everyone the same all the time. He was actually happy for Randy. He knew God was already moving in his life.

When they finished setting up, Randy began to get the supper meal ready. Some of the boys, including Roberto and Juanito, stepped up to offer to help him with the work. He accepted quickly, and with a smile. Together they walked to a small rivulet, crystal clear as it ran apparently from the mountains further north. It wasn't wide or deep, but it was clean and there was plenty of it. The boys whose job it was to care for the mules had already removed their burdens and had headed a bit downstream that they could allow them to drink. Josiah was already down there with Mustgofast. He had already had his fill and was nibbling on the tender shoots of green grass by the water. Josiah had pulled the brush from his backpack and was stroking his glistening sides and neck. The mustang was enjoying himself immensely. You did not have to be an expert to pick up on it.

A line had been strung for the animals. It would not do to have them frightened away by some howling coyote, or any animal, and it was clear that they took comfort in not being too far apart.

Josiah decided he would keep Mustgofast with him until it was time to eat, unless Mr. Jack told him to do differently.

Christopher came over to tell him that they could go exploring close by and they would just return to camp when they heard the clang of the metal rod against the triangle.

Quickly Josiah ran back to put the brush away, and he and Mustgofast followed behind the boys. Only the cooks and the adults stayed in the camp. Some of the boys headed upstream while others followed the little brook down along its winding course. Many of the boys asked about the gold specks glistening on the bottom and those who had traveled out west the previous year were quick to fill them in.

"It's just fools' gold," said Brian. "Don't be taken in by it. It isn't real."

Josiah responded simply, "Some of it is."

"Well, that sure is true," answered Pete, who had come up behind them. "And I know some people in a little village in Iraq who can vouch for that."

A warm feeling filled the heart of Josiah as he thought back on God's provision for the Kurds. He knew they needed far more, but it was a start. And, after all, isn't that what this trip was about: God's provision?

Chapter Fifteen

Amazing Grace

What a great night that first night was. It seemed as though everyone had worked up an appetite for their beans, beef jerky, pickles, and bread. And, of course, there was the water; plenty of icy cold water.

The darkness seemed to come in quickly. The relaxed atmosphere amongst friends was like a sedative. The four boys, almost simultaneously, realized how tired they were. It seemed the change of time zones was just telling on them. They could barely keep their eyes opened.

"I have to go to bed," offered Cameron, with no embarrassment. "Man, all of a sudden I am exhausted."

Quickly the others agreed with him, and, though they felt badly to break off early from the festivities, it seemed they had no choice. Josiah said honestly, "If I don't go now, I think someone will have to carry me."

They excused themselves and made their way happily to the tents which seemed to be calling out their names like some sweet lullaby.

Josiah was the first in their little tent. He meant to wait until Zach came in to discuss their first day of traveling, but his good intentions were lost to the overpowering call from that stronger voice: sleep. Quickly he drifted into that place where dreams become reality, and, even as they had done many times before, he and Mustgofast were flying effortlessly across an open meadow. Overhead an eagle soared, but for all the wind currents, and with his greatest effort, he could not keep up with the speed of the mustang and his boy.

Zach came into the tent and knew immediately by the evenness of Siah's breathing that he was already gone. He didn't mind though, for it would have been difficult for him to hold any conversation, though there were so many things he wanted to share with his brother about the day. He knew they could wait. Off in the distance he could hear the softness of Pete's guitar. The last thought he had before drifting off to sleep was that if he could have chosen to be anywhere in the world at this moment, this is the place he would have chosen.

None of the four could believe that the next thing they heard was the sound of Juanito's shofar. As though it cried out from another land, the resonance of the voice of it masterfully separated the night from the day. There was something special about knowing that in the Bible the voice of God was referred to as the voice of the trumpet, or the shofar. It seemed to demand a response, and, for sure, received one from the four boys.

Quickly, and in disbelief, they rose from their slumber, shocked to find the sun shining brightly and sparkling like so many diamonds and crystals against the glistening dew on the green grass.

As they looked around, the boys saw that basically all the other boys had still been sleeping. They felt better as they would not be the last to rise.

"My goodness, did I sleep!" said Chris with an impish look of guilt on his face. "Am I the only one who was so tired? All of a sudden it hit me last night and I just couldn't stay awake."

"Oh, you're sure not alone," answered one of the boys who had overheard him from his group. I was flat out beat myself."

Quickly they all changed and made their way to the fresh cold mountain water to make ready for the day. The morning was crisp and pleasantly cool.

They were told by Randy that they could eat first as the animals would be fine until they finished. Josiah, however, could not resist going to Mustgofast to greet him a good morning. "You were in my dreams again, my friend," he whispered to the horse so that no one else would hear him. "We were flying across the meadow and it was a day just like today. It was wonderful! That old eagle I saw yesterday was trying to catch up with us, but there was just no way he could manage; not even with the wind currents on his side. No, Mustgofast, he was no match for your speed. It wasn't even close."

The little mustang warmed to the sound of the voice of the one he considered to be his master. Even as

Josiah remembered so fondly of last year, Mustgofast made sounds as though he was talking to him, and, indeed he may has well have been, for Josiah understood plainly every word.

Juanito and Roberto joined the four boys as soon as they came back from the water's edge into the camp site. Already they had become close friends in spite of the language difference. The four were excited that they too were a part of the tribe of Levi.

Breakfast was ready to be served. Of course it was no different from last night's meal. Nevertheless, everyone was hungry, and, when you're hungry you are not picky.

Mr. Jack made his way over to Josiah as he was chewing on the last of his beef jerky. "Man," he whispered, "I sure could use a big old glass of cold orange juice, Josiah. Whose idea was this anyway? Was there really any need to take it to this extreme, my friend?" Smiling, he continued, "I see a little of your Meme' coming out in you, and I can't in all honesty say it's the side I like the best of her." Everyone laughed.

It didn't take long to finish their morning meal. In spite of the fact that it was beans, bread, and beef jerky, all were pleasantly filled when they were done.

"Let's get our gear packed," said Pete. "It's time to move out of Succoth. We want to figure to be on the trail not much after seven every morning."

Everyone scurried in anticipation, even the adults, to get the gear rolled up and packed onto the animals so they might be on their way. Though it had only been one day, it seemed already they had the routine down regarding whose day it was to care for the mules.

"Oh, look!" shouted one of the boys, pointing across the plane to the edge of the tree line, "is that an elk?"

Momentarily the great elk with his expansive antlers stood at alert from the shout and then bounded into the sparse woods behind him. "It sure was," said Randy. "And he was a big one at that. That boy has been around for a few years."

Zachary suddenly remembered to hang his camera around his neck in case he had an opportunity to get more photos. There was no way though, that he would have gotten a picture of the elk, for he was clearly not in the mood to stand around and pose.

"We're going to have a great day," whispered Josiah to Mustgofast. "I can feel it already."

It was a well-rested group that turned to the East from Succoth that day after joining hands in prayer. They had no idea how far they would be traveling; they were just happy to be on the move. They wanted Pete to surprise them with what came next.

Zachary tried his best to pan the group in the video mode of his camera. Mr. Jack was looking around as he was advising him and giving him pointers regarding what he felt would represent the best shots. Of course Mr. Jack himself took photos and videos constantly, as was his way. Zach was at his peak.

Everyone held his staff in front of him. It really was a marvelous sight to see. Only the women did not carry staffs. For the sake of authenticity, Randy had left them off the list in the making of them. The women didn't mind though; in fact, they felt strangely good and somehow sheltered by it.

The two camera buffs zoomed in on such things as boys leading mules and Randy masterfully driving the little supply wagon. They even took some stupendous close-ups of grasshoppers in flight, crickets, and butterflies retracting nectar from their hostesses.

The whole scene was really rather pleasing to the eyes and warmed the hearts of all who were a part of it. In a sense it was very different from last year's tour, Mr. Jack thought. It somehow carried with it a feeling of nostalgia, as though it were almost struggling to reach something buried deep in the heart.

All walked in silence for a time, as though they had previously agreed upon it, in an attitude, it seemed, of quiet meditation. It was not somber or sad at all, but peaceful and contented, like a good and healing silence.

It was Mrs. Patty who finally quietly spoke. "I remember," she said, "a couple of years ago hearing someone playing "Amazing Grace" on a woodwind instrument. I couldn't describe then, and I can't now, what that melody did to me. But, whatever it was, I feel the same way now. Somehow the solo from that instrument didn't just bring me to tears, but touched something inside of me that desperately wanted only to please the LORD. It is like the sweetest symphony that filters through the deepest part of me." And, with that, she said no more.

Mr. Jack thought to himself, "I couldn't have said it better, my love."

Chapter Sixteen

All-purpose Clouds and Fire

The boys were surprised at how quickly the time passed. They had not stopped at all when, off in the distance, someone spotted a sign. "It's another stopping place!" shouted the boy named James from the tribe of Dan.

"Well, I guess the Danites have this one," smiled Pete, almost inviting a friendly competition. "Can you read the name on the sign?"

"Not yet!" shouted James.

"What are you waiting for?" whispered Mr. Jack to Josiah. "We can't get beat by the Danites. It's bad enough they spotted the sign first."

Josiah took off with Mustgofast right beside him. He had a sudden urge to throw himself onto his friend's back and have some real fun, but, of course he did not give in to it. He had already been told beforehand that he must walk like the rest. There would be no free rides. After all, this whole thing had been his idea.

"It says, '**Etham**', Mr. Jack!" he yelled back. He had taken the other boys unaware when he bolted, and clearly some of the older, much bigger ones might have beaten him to the spot, but he had the advantage of surprise on his side and he was a great sprinter. There was no doubt in anyone's mind that after this stopping place, everyone would be on the lookout to be the first to the next marker.

It was late morning. The two stopping places had not been far apart. Everyone gathered around the sign to get their journeyman's card.

"Let's all sit down a minute and enjoy a piece of jerky and listen to the story of Etham. This place," Mr. Jack began, "was on the edge of the wilderness at the bottom of the Arabian Gulf.

It was an isolated desert place, which is probably why its precise location has been lost. There was obviously nothing much going on here. It was an introduction, so to speak, of a type of separation from the rest of the world; perhaps even a bit frightening because of the stark difference from the Egypt the Jew had just left, even as it might be for us walking away from the familiar. The adrenaline surge from the first night had worn off, no doubt, and the uncertainty of life ahead in unfamiliar surroundings would begin to set in. It probably did not look much like an adventure to them. There were no shopping malls, arcades, bells, or whistles.

Yes, they had been reintroduced to God. They had experienced His deliverance and witnessed His mighty hand against the Egyptians. But, aside from the familiar faces of their brethren, this place would have seemed to hold little appeal.

They probably didn't mind as much as you may think however, because, remember, they didn't plan on being here long anyhow. They were only passing through, not setting down roots; after all, they were headed for the land of milk and honey. For that they could tolerate the seclusion of this place."

It was in Etham that our big brother Israel first experienced another facet of God's provision and guidance. It is here that the Bible first mentions the pillar of cloud that the LORD provided to show them the way by day, and a pillar of fire to give them light and lead them by night.

Listen carefully, please," Mr. Jack continued. "We are not talking about a wispy cloud like we see billowing overhead now, or a bonfire that gives a bit of light from its ground position when you are close enough to it. The pillar literally refers to a broad column, reaching from heaven to earth; a supernatural monolith of sorts, for you sci-fi fans.

The cloud by day no doubt would not only guide them, for they wouldn't move unless the cloud did, but sheltered them against the blistering hot rays of the mid-eastern sun.

The nights could get very cold and so the pillar of fire would not only direct them when they traveled and provide them with light throughout the night; that is, the whole camp, but also warm them."

He stopped for a moment while everyone seemed to mull over the words he had spoken. "Just imagine," he continued, "what it must have looked like. It represented the presence of God to this group; a roadmap in the wilderness to be followed to their destination. One day, in heaven, I hope to see a replay of that footage. It must have been magnificent. I don't think most of our reading does it justice, or we would be far more excited about it. That I can state beyond a shadow of a doubt.

We will break for camp here. It is part of God's plan; a period of quiet reflection away from the initial hyper-surge and a kind of dip into reality. The fear of the unknown and the lack of trust have driven many a Christian back to Egypt. Sometimes the known, even if it is not pleasant, can have more appeal than the unknown, so, back into that endless grave we crawl, and many never get their hands on the promises of God. Christianity is the greatest adventure on planet earth. Mark it down! You heard it right here in Etham at the border of the wilderness, if you've never heard it before."

Many had gotten out their notepads and were scribbling even as they had in Succoth, those things that Mr. Jack shared with them. They surmised that in the looking back, these would actually take on even more meaning.

So punctuated was Mr. Jack's speech and so zealous his attitude that most, including the adults, looked skyward to see if there might be a cloud forming on this beautifully clear day.

"Today, between Succoth and Etham, is the Suez Canal, but, of course that wasn't opened until 1869. It connects the Mediterranean Sea to the Red Sea. It took more than a decade to construct and is just over one hundred miles long.

What do you say we set up camp before we do anything else?" he suggested. "It's a beautiful day to have some fun. Surely, though probably not this early in their trip, our Jewish brothers must have done a few fun things. Certainly their youth must have been allowed to explore in their spare time."

Inspired now, everyone got to work.

The boys talked about with what precision Pete must have chosen this spot. Southwest they could see a tree line where it looked like just beyond there might be a major body of water; perhaps a river. To the East it was dry and barren looking; rather drab and not too exciting, and northwest there was the last green meadow they had crossed. Of course they were headed east; that's where the Promised Land was.

Josiah said it was as though God had designed this place for just this time that they could come close to duplicating the authentic experience. No doubt, He probably had other reasons, but He certainly knew that they would gather here one day. Of that Josiah was certain. And, as far as he was concerned, it was great.

After setting up and relieving the animals of their burdens, they were told that they could walk southwest toward the water line. They could spend some time there after allowing the animals to drink. The leaders would go with them.

For the sake of the experience the campsite had not been set up on the shores of whatever body of water that might be, for it would have lost something, for Etham had not been a coastal place. It would be better to camp here tonight, slightly northeast, with the animals tied nearby, away from the running water.

"Maybe we should change into shorts," suggested one of the leaders. "It's getting pretty hot out here, and since we're not really traveling, maybe we'll have a chance to get into the water. Would that be OK, Jack?"

"Sounds like a plan to me," Mr. Jack answered quickly. "Water is always a great entertainer. After lunch we will have the afternoon free."

Almost everyone scurried to get into something lighter than their heavy dungarees. It didn't take long before all of them had joined ranks to move south. Staffs in hand, they headed in a grand procession for the water.

It seemed odd to the boys that there was so much walking involved, for from their vantage point it looked to be very close. Somehow, however, there must have been some sort of mirage involved as at least fifteen minutes passed before they could actually see any of the water from the river.

This body of water was wider and more forceful than yesterday's rivulet, but it appeared just as clear. The bottom could be seen in greatest detail. The little wave peaks looked to be smiling up at the source of their light, the sun, while the ripples moving downstream joined them, actually laughing out loud, or so it seemed to Josiah. He knew that if he were able to make mention of his observation to Mustgofast, that the little mustang would be in total agreement with him. Of course, he could not, for someone would no doubt be listening, and he would have none of that. Some conversations were simply not to be thrown out carelessly.

At the mouth of the river they had had to cross a plateau of jagged rocks that looked like it had somehow become separated from its parent figures.

From beneath this plateau which stood high above the otherwise fairly level ground sprung forth this river. "Hey," said Cameron to the boys, "doesn't this look like the book that Meme' wrote on **Living Waters from the Rock That is Higher Than I**? It seems like the water flows right out from the rock. You can't even see where it's coming from, but it gets deeper as it leaves the source. Imagine the force that must be pushing behind it for it to be able to do that?"

Mr. Jack was impressed by his astute observation and the simple explanation that seemed to tie in with that great Biblical concept.

Chapter Seventeen

A Personal Pentecost

A short way down the waterway was a relatively deep pool that seemed to be hollowed from years of swirling waters, much like a whirlpool. The waters did not appear so strong that the whirlpool would draw and hold anyone beneath the surface, but were more like the moving waters of a health spa. The bottom seemed to be about five feet below the surface of the water.

The group couldn't wait until after they had had their lunch that they might come back and dive into the beckoning waters. The overall scene was very inviting. Even the adults were looking forward to it for the day had turned out to be sweltering hot.

The tribes walked south along the banks of the river on both sides. The shores in some areas were as much as one to one hundred, fifty feet apart, but the downstream flow was gentle and the water did not appear to be extremely deep or treacherous. In the half-mile they walked they saw no whitewater. More than once they saw a fish cut the surface of the water. At one point a beautiful rainbow trout appeared almost as though he could fly; suspended in mid-air, frozen for a split-second before dropping back down.

"He's just showing off," laughed Randy. "He wouldn't do that if I had my pole. I'll have to remember this spot for another time. I'd totally forgotten how beautiful the northern part of this river is. It's been so long since I've even been up here. Sylvie and I used to fish this area. That girl sure loved to fish," he said reminiscently. "Many times she'd put me to shame."

Off in the distance they could hear the sound of the clanging dinner call. Randy wondered who had prepared the midday meal. He was glad to be where he was though; it was like memory therapy. It was time. He had been vegetating and simply going through the motions long enough.

"My God, breathe on me, again" he said aloud.

The simple, open, and honest prayer touched Mr. Jack and he almost wept.

Randy was not feeling sorry for himself, but it was rather as though he had just been awakened from a long time sleep; a type of hibernation. He suddenly noticed that those within earshot had become quiet and sensed that he had spoken aloud. He hadn't meant to, but he did not apologize.

He walked the few feet that separated him from Jack and like a brother put his hand upon Jack's shoulder. "I need my own personal Pentecost, and I know that God wants to give it to me," he said, smiling through watery eyes. "And, I mean to have it. It is long overdue; shame on me. There'll be no more wallowing. Thank you so much, Jack, for your inspiration of this exodus trip. Rather than walking away from something, though, I feel like I'm coming back to where I took a detour and turned away a few years back.

You see, Sylvie and I were already enjoying life in the Promised Land. I walked back into the wilderness after the LORD called her home. I didn't plan to; it just happened. I didn't recognize the face of that particular enemy in the land of milk and honey, but, glory to God, I do now. Thank you again."

"Don't thank me," Jack answered honestly. "This whole thing is Josiah's idea. I just put some feet on the plan. Guess I'm pretty good at doing that. The inspiration behind it though, comes from that ten-year-old boy over there with a heart for the things that really matter. I hope he doesn't lose that as he grows older. I pray he sees it as a gift from God to be guarded and treasured jealously."

Twenty-five minutes later they were all sitting to a welcome spread of beans, bread, and beef jerky. It was hot in this particular spot so no one was quite as hungry as they might have been had the day been cool. Most all of them had their minds fixed on the beckoning pool twenty minutes away and couldn't wait to finish and clean up that they might be on their way to the water park just over the mirage to the southwest. Mustgofast cropped the tender grass as he waited patiently for his boy. Josiah knew that the horse was as excited as he was about returning to the water. He knew that it would be a fun afternoon. As soon as everyone finished, each was responsible for bringing their own bowls and utensils to the spot set aside for cleaning.

Together the ladies washed and dried everything and stored it away in the wooden crates in the wagon. They insisted that no men should do this cleaning if only for the sake of authenticity. Besides that, they enjoyed their time together as twelve women gathered, laughed, and chatted about the up-to-date happenings in their groups. It was a fun time they had no intention of being deprived of.

The ladies marveled that none of the guys even made an attempt to move out toward the water without them. Somehow, they felt respected, and it felt good.

In no time it seemed the tribes were headed back to the water. For compassion's sake the boys led the mules back toward the water where they might have some relief from the high overbearing heat of the sun. They could be tethered on the shaded side of the rock that plateaued high above the ground's surface and be very comfortable. In the wagon were some portable tethering pins which simply had to be screwed into the ground to hold the animal within the range of his lead rope. Someone had thought of everything.

Only Mustgofast was allowed by his master to roam free, for, of the animals, only Mustgofast could be trusted.

It didn't take long for everyone to be in the water; the boys' shirts, boots, socks, hats, and staffs, left on the shore. The water was surprisingly cold. The leaders were the first in, even as they had organized earlier, for it was for them to test the waters. They inched toward the whirling pool to discover if it had the potential to hold anyone captive. Remarkably the water here was several degrees warmer than that which was in the shallower areas. It was an odd phenomenon which seemed to make no sense to them.

"This really is like a spa!" shouted back one of the boys following closely behind his leader. "It's nice and warm!"

No one needed more of an invitation than that as the huge pool came alive, teeming with happy campers. Juanito smiled at Josiah and through his translator said, "Pete thought of everything. This is great!"

What fun they had that afternoon. They traveled the limit of their allowance as they were told to go no further than one mile south, according to the calculation of their leaders. Though they swam together, when any leader moved down or upstream, each of the boys from that tribe had to follow.

"We've been to waterparks that weren't this much fun," said Zach to the boys. After a couple of hours of swimming, wading, and exploring, some of the leaders sat on the banks watching their groups. No one made an attempt to go back to Etham as this place was so perfect.

Mr. Jack sat on the shore, his wife beside him, as they watched Pete horsing around with the boys, and Randy who was cupping his hands and allowing some of the smaller boys to use him as a launch for diving.

Several times some of the boys came forward to Mr. Randy; the most knowledgeable in the group regarding such things, with golden-specked rocks that they hoped might be real gold. All of them, however, had been pronounced as fool's gold by the master.

Mr. Jack suggested that those who wanted might take a short nap so that maybe they could hang out a little later at night, enjoying their time together. Several were sound asleep on the grassy banks of the river beneath the shade of the trees looming, gangly but full overhead. Zach and Mr. Jack were taking photos of the activities including the sleepers.

Mr. Jack thought the scene looked like an advertisement for a 'yet-to-be-discovered' remote resort where peace-of-mind can still be found. "What a powerful advertising brochure this would make," he said to Zach. "We'll call it **A Personal Pentecost**."

Finally, as the afternoon wore on, the groups began to head back to the campsite, exhausted from the strenuous activity in the water. It was still very hot, but they felt refreshed from the fresh cool water.

Chapter Eighteen

Strange Logic

The four boys felt rested that night, as all of them had been amongst those who had taken a short nap. After supper they formed a large circle around a fire that Pete had kindled, for the temperature had already dropped considerably. Everyone felt the blessing of being part of the group. Off in the distance the coyotes howled as Pete and Brian played their guitars.

A couple of the boys joined the two with harmonicas. Zach took a little video footage and more photos. "My dad will love these pictures," he whispered to Roberto who was sitting beside him. "He'll be so jealous he wasn't actually on the trip to take some pictures himself. He just eats this stuff up. I have to admit, I like it a lot myself."

Zach waited for the delayed response from Roberto, for, of course, everything had to be translated. Roberto came from a different world down there in Mexico City. He couldn't imagine at eleven years old, owning a camera as fancy as the one that Zach had.

"Well, Siah," whispered Mr. Jack to his friend, "thanks again. We could be sitting around this fire with hot chocolate and marshmallows, but, of course those things would be out-of-place in the wilderness. Yep, thanks a lot, Buddy."

Matter-of-factly, Josiah simply responded with a big smile on his face, "You're welcome, Mr. Jack. That's what friends are for."

As soon as a few from the group began to file to their tents for the night, the four boys rose to their feet to follow suit. They were tired. They had talked it over and decided it wasn't worth being tired all day in order to stay up a little later at night. That just didn't make sense to any of them. They excused themselves, said their good-nights, and headed for their tents. Tomorrow would come soon enough.

The next morning, all of them arose before the shofar sounded. All four stood beside Juanito as he sounded the call to rise. Again, it seemed every noise that had been heard previously, halted at the voice of the call. Even the insects ceased their endless monotone of sounds for a time.

In minutes the camp was alive with activity. No one would be sorry to leave this spot. It wasn't that it had been a horrible experience, in fact, it had been great. They hoped that the next stop might offer a little more variety in the way of colors and sights. Most of the group would have agreed; tan and brown, stones and sand, really didn't hold the promise of much adventure. Even as Josiah had suggested in his original email to Mr. Jack though, *no one would be allowed to complain* as the Israelites had. Everyone, including the leaders, had agreed by way of their word, that they would abide by this simple rule of attitude. After all, unlike the Israelites, they had the advantage of knowing what position their complaining had put them in. Here they were looking to come into their heritage; not to be disinherited.

"It's a shame to be walking away from that beautiful river spot down in the southwest; don't you agree?" began Mr. Jack when he had everyone's attention.

Everyone signified agreement with a loud, "Amen!"

"The Israelites knew that the land of promise, Canaan, lay directly to the East of this land, even as it does for us. But, again, they were not free to choose their own route, especially since the LORD had provided the beacon of clouds and fire. That's kinda' hard to argue against."

Again, everyone nodded in agreement.

"And, remember, the goal was the destination, not the trip there. They had had a long enough vacation. It was time to go home."

Randy alone shouted a loud, "Amen!" to that. Though he had a big smile on his face, the response was tenderly heartbreaking to those who understood the depth of that single word of commitment; Mr. Jack probably as much as anyone else.

"Randy, my friend," he said. "We're going home."

Mrs. Patty had a very difficult time keeping her emotions under wrap.

As Mr. Jack struggled to gain composure the voice of the shofar split the air. Juanito had moved to take it out of its case, to raise it to his lips, and to blow the sound of three short and one long.

At that moment, Mr. Jack realized that he certainly wasn't the only one moved by the plight of Mr. Random Mann. The sight of many brought to tears by the sound of the voice of the shofar indicated that neither was it simply he and Juanito. Already, in just these few days, they were as a family, caring deeply about the welfare of the others, even without having everything spelled out to them.

"This is the way God meant it to be," continued Mr. Jack, when sufficient time had passed, "a people moved under the sensitivity and unction of the Holy Spirit. This is as good as it gets this side of heaven. I'm sure we have much to learn on this journey, but it is clear that we have already learned one of the greatest lessons offered in this life. It has to do with relationship. Only the heart can receive and teach it, for the mind and flesh can never ascend to it. It cannot be duplicated by anything as plastic as the flesh. The lock on the door to real relationship was opened and the doorway made available by the blood of our Jesus.

That is why we try to open doors in the Mideast by forming relationships and bonds of trust with the hurting nation of Kurds. It is something that, given time, will prove itself, for the basis of it is love.

The enemy can't touch it, for it is outside of his reach. God knows he has been trying from the beginning, but like the flesh, he does not hold the key to open the door. If we maintain our relationship with God and with each other, he is powerless against us.

Sometimes a demonstration of the testimony of hands is necessary to prove the intention of the heart. If we would try that more often, I personally believe that the gospel would have more of a platform to succeed in the land; any land."

Of course, there was no arguing that kind of logic, for it was logic based on experience and Mr. Jack's own testimony. For that matter, why would any in this group even care to argue against it?

"The LORD has spoken to me," said Mr. Jack, switching to his role as Moses. "He has said that we must turn back. Not as in a 'go back to Egypt turn', but more like a one hundred, twenty degree course change. He has said that rather than continue southeast, (remember, He is not going to lead us through the land of the Philistine warriors which would be directly east) He wants us to turn toward the water and travel south along its western bank. Of course in the day of the Israelites, this would have been the Red Sea.

Now, you must know that the Jew might have had a bit of a time with this directive. Why, after all, would God desire to put a sea between them and the land of promise directly to the East? At some point, of course, they would have to cross it. Why would God direct them away from the place of their destination? That didn't make a lot of sense.

Was this Moses character really hearing from God or making it up as he went? Of course, you and I read the story and can discern God's reasoning. They did not have the script to rehearse or to read back on. Again, there is that carnal logic that becomes our enemy, actually blocking our ears to the voice of God. What purpose would it serve to turn back?

And so," Mr. Jack continued, "we shall turn back toward the West banks of this river and head south along its shore."

Before they left camp they joined hands and prayed, thanking God for their night in Etham, for the cloud and fire of guidance and protection, covering and shelter. "You are a good Father," prayed Mr. Jack, "Your mercy continuing even when we fail to notice or acknowledge. Thank You, LORD," he ended simply.

Everyone lifted up a quiet, "Amen."

The eleven tribes followed the tribe of Levi, led by Moses, that is, Mr. Jack, away from Etham toward the South and along the Western bank of the river that flowed from the rock.

Chapter Nineteen

A Story to Tell

Even as they had the first day, they traveled most of this third day, into the late afternoon stopping only at short intervals. Pete seemed driven to make it to the next stopping place by a certain time. Perhaps he had the schedule planned precisely, though it wasn't like him to be quite so rigid.

"We want to make it to the campsite by at least five o'clock," he said. "Let's see if we can pick up the pace a little."

As they traveled the shore of the river, the sun beat down strongly, but there was a bit of a breeze from the East blowing across the water. It was not unpleasant. The temperature seemed to be at least fifteen degrees less than yesterday's. For that they were thankful.

They had passed many spots that looked like they might be worth exploring, and the boys of course noticed all of them. They didn't know if it was for the sake of the discipline of it, or if perhaps there might be another reason that Pete wasn't allowing them a little adventure time. After all, they reasoned, it was still light at six or seven o'clock and even at eight. What difference should it make if they were off schedule by an hour or two? It would take only minutes to set up camp. Suffice it to say though, that no one complained. They knew better!

It was just after four when one of the boys from the tribe of Judah spotted the sign identifying the next stopping place. "There it is!" he yelled and took off to be the first there.

"I guess Judah has this one," said Josiah to Mr. Jack, who, for some reason, didn't even encourage Josiah to try to claim the name. Perhaps he surmised that his young friend was tired after a full day of walking.

Let the reader know that Siah wasn't simply walking. Even as he did with every outdoor activity, he threw himself into it. Sometimes after a day of fun at home, for example, Josiah would actually be physically sick, for he would spend himself so entirely for whatever cause or activity he deemed worth the adventure. He knew nothing of the casual laid-back approach in certain areas; that would have been a contradiction to the zeal that pulsed through him (save that for school). Besides, Mr. Jack knew that the day wasn't over yet.

"The sign says **Pihahiroth**," shouted Shawn from the tribe of Judah to Mr. Jack.

When they all arrived at the spot, a short distance west of the banks of the river, he suggested they sit down for a moment as someone handed out the journeyman's cards.

"Finally," he started, "we have come to the third night's stopping place. We find ourselves on strangely what seems the wrong side of the river's shores. But, the LORD has directed me, Moses, to stop here between Migdol and the Pihahiroth near the Red Sea. We are still in the land of Egypt.

It would seem that God is not done with the Egyptians yet. He hasn't dealt with their offenses to the point where He could say to Himself that He had avenged His Own. He is the One Who decides when vengeance has been satisfied, for it is His honor, His Word, and His people who have been challenged. Let the Father decide for His children. It really works out best that way.

God's was a plan; not an experiment. His children are not up for grabs by the enemy.

Pihahiroth literally means the voice from the mouth of a cavern. It means to bore down into the crevice of the serpent or the cell of a prison. How significant is that? It is not a place that one would venture unprotected, unless he is a fool. And if one is protected, Satan becomes the fool when he dares to crawl out of his cave after the one who is serving God, thinking even for one moment, that he may come out the victor."

The adults in particular were held spellbound by Mr. Jack's definition for it carried more than just a little meaning to each of them.

"Remember," Mr. Jack continued, "we, like the Israelites, are battling two enemies: the flesh and Satan.

It is in this place that God will deal with the Pharaoh, a type of Satan in our lives, and show him that God is LORD. God was not worried; He had set the whole thing up. After His Own left Egypt, He again hardened the heart of the Pharaoh that he might experience firsthand the power of the God who would vindicate for His firstborn, Israel. God meant to be given honor by the Pharaoh and the Egyptians.

Before we continue, let me suggest that we set up camp right here, rest for half-an-hour, and then have a bite to eat at about six o'clock."

Everyone complied willingly as they placed their cards in their backpacks and followed their leaders to set up for the night. It seemed like a good plan.

Even though they were tired, however, the boys were casing out the spots that they wanted to explore later on if time permitted. They could almost taste the adventure in this spot.

It wasn't long before they were awakened by the sound of the clang of the dinner call.

Was it already six o'clock?

They hurried outside their tents to find others doing the same; most appearing to have just been awakened as well. The short nap had revived them somewhat and they felt they were ready for the rest of the day, whatever that might be.

Everyone sat on the bank of the river to eat the now-very-familiar repast of beans, pickles, bread, jerky, and water. Josiah had to admit to himself that a grilled hotdog would have tasted nice right about now, but, in all honesty, he really wasn't feeling too badly about it. Immediately his mind went to the Kurdistan people and he prayed that they would turn to Jesus and that He would supernaturally meet their needs, providing food, shelter, and salvation for them.

By six-thirty everyone had finished eating and the utensils and dishes were being brought back to the spot where the ladies had set up for cleaning them.

"We'll wait for the girls," suggested Mr. Jack, "before we hear a little more about this third stopping place." The ladies took their cue and quickened the pace a bit so as not to hold up the group.

Everyone was seated now, except for Mr. Jack, who, with staff in hand, had just begun to speak, "Just imagine," he began. The cloud has been moving ahead of us and has stopped right here in this place. We know, by God's Word, that He had hardened the Pharaoh's heart, but the Israelites did not know this. Moses of course knew, but he had no clue what to expect. Here we are: two to three million people if not more."

Suddenly, as Mr. Jack spoke, the sound of thundering hooves against the ground could be heard off in the distance. "What's that?" asked Mr. Jack of the tribes.

"Someone's coming!" answered one of the leaders.

"It looks like a sizable group of men on horses."

"Good thing this isn't Biblical times," said Josiah to Mr. Jack, "or it would be the Egyptians."

Clearly whoever was coming was headed in their direction. Everyone grew quiet. There was almost something scary about it. As they drew closer it appeared there were about forty horses coming strong and fast and bearing down on them.

"It looks like the Egyptians!" shouted Pete.

All of the riders appeared to be wearing the typical clothing of the Egyptians including the loose robes and the cloth head coverings.

One of the leaders from the tribe of Asher approached Mr. Jack and seemed to be in a panic. "What?" he said, raising his voice, "there weren't enough graves in Egypt, Moses? You took us out here to die?"

Another yelled as the horses closed the distance between them and Pihahiroth, "It would have been better if you had left us there in Egypt to serve the Egyptians than to take us out here in the wilderness."

Now real panic began to sweep through the camp as the sound of approaching hoof beats drew nearer. Josiah wanted to stand up and run away; it was so real.

"Shh!" said Mr. Jack, his arm outstretched holding his staff, "be still and see the salvation of the LORD. The Egyptians that you see today, you will see no more forever.

Be still, for the LORD your God shall fight this battle for you. It is His. And," he continued, more softly now, "imagine, if you will; the LORD spoke to Moses to tell the people to move forward toward the Red Sea.

And so, fold up your tents and gear quickly. We are moving out!" The forty horsemen were getting closer. Everyone hurried; the air electric with the tension of the unfolding drama. The boys knew, of course, that these were not really Egyptians, but somehow their clothing and this place by the water charged them with purpose. They could not talk themselves out of it.

Like a seasoned army the boys and their leaders formed ranks and awaited their orders from Mr. Jack.

"The LORD has told me to lift up my rod and to stretch my hand out over the sea and that he would part it and that Israel would walk across on dry ground.

Of course I can't duplicate that, but look behind us, the Egyptians are here!" Some of the boys and their leaders actually screamed.

There they were, on their horses, looking formidable and as scary as the enemy himself.

"We've got the Israelites trapped!" shouted one of the men from his horse. "They can't move south; the terrain is too rough and we'll be on them before they get anywhere. They won't be going east, obviously, the water will stop them. They've trapped themselves!" The group of Egyptians laughed at their predicament.

"And now," continued Mr. Jack, "imagine, if you will, the Angel Who has been leading us in the pillar of cloud, takes up the rear flank, between us and the Egyptians. Suddenly it is as though the darkest night has just swept upon them, and we, the Israelites have the light of day to cross the Red Sea.

Remember, they were not forty men on horseback. They were a seasoned army of the Pharaoh's greatest. There were six hundred of the best chariots that he could lay his hands on, plus all the other chariots in Egypt. There were his finest horses, fast and strong, driven by expert horsemen. There were captains known for their military savvy who led the troops of men; all with blood in their eyes and vengeance in their hearts."

"Hey!" one of the forty men on the horses shouted, "I can't see a thing! Where did this thick blackness suddenly come from?"

"They can see nothing, and we cannot see them, so thick and dark is the pillar of cloud. We are not really interested in them, though, we just want to get to the other shore of this deep wide sea.

[3] *And Moses stretched out his hand over the sea; and the LORD caused the sea to go back by a strong east wind all that night, and made the sea dry land, and the waters were divided.*

And the children of Israel went into the midst of the sea upon the dry ground: and the waters were a wall unto them on their right hand, and on their left."

Mr. Jack quoted the text from the Bible. "Come now," he said, "let us move across the water." And so they crossed. They moved in ranks and were told there was no need to panic, for God would not remove His blinding presence from the Egyptians until His Own were safe and sound on the other shore.

Though the shores were a good distance apart, the water was shallow here with a rocky bottom where people and animals alike were at little risk in crossing.

---

[3] Exodus 14: 21-22

"At this point," continued Mr. Jack, "let your imagination run wild. This is another portion of history I would like to catch on the re-runs; a high wall of water being held back on either side by the wind at the command of God. And the ground would not have been soupy, but dry. The Word says it very clearly. He caused the wind to dry up the wet ground so His people could cross without mishap. There would have been no need to hurry and panic for the Egyptians would not be going anywhere until the darkness was lifted. How could they?"

Even though Mr. Jack had said there was no reason to rush, the tribes felt an urgency. Then, when they were safely on the other side, they turned to look back at the forty strangers who were now standing by their horses as though paralyzed.

"By the time the Israelites made it all the way across, it was early the next morning," said Mr. Jack, "for there were many of them. There was no problem though, for on this side, all night long, they were guided by the pillar of fire. It may as well have been midday.

Then, God lifted the cloud from the midst of the Egyptians. As soon as they saw the Israelites on the other shore they pursued after them like a child after a lollipop; the best and strongest of Egypt's royal chariots and the warriors on their horses against the seemingly defenseless Israelites. I mean, come on, did they not notice the wall of water on either side? Were they so blinded by their hatred or hardened in their hearts that they didn't even wonder about this whole scene?"

Screaming now in an angry rage, even as one voice, the forty riders mounted their horses and headed into the water. It was terrifying.

"Again, imagine this to be a dry roadway between two walls of water. They are almost here." And, so they were and again fear gripped the twelve tribes on Mr. Jack's side.

"Just as they almost reach this shore the LORD looks through the pillar of fire and the cloud and troubles the Egyptians. He takes the wheels from their chariots and they are driven heavily into the ground, no doubt, sending the occupants flying to the ground. It is then that their eyes are opened. God had said this would come to pass that they would realize Who He was."

At this point two of the lead riders, almost to the other shore jumped from their horses into the water. One shouted to the men behind, "Let us go back, from the face of Israel, for the LORD fights their battle against the Egyptians!"

"But it was too late," picked up Mr. Jack, "even though they tried to turn back. The LORD told me, Moses, to stretch my hand out upon the sea and the waters closed in upon the Egyptians, every one, and by morning every chariot, every horse and horseman, had been swallowed up by the sea. Not so much as one remained.

It was not shallow water like we see here. The Word tells us that they sank to the bottom like stones and the depths of the waters covered over them; even the finest chariots and the most valiant soldiers. And in the morning many of their bodies washed up on the shore."

The forty horsemen turned their horses and left the way they had come, without so much as another word. It seemed somehow fitting and very obviously part of the dramatic presentation set up by Pete. No wonder he had wanted them to make this stopping place at a particular time.

He had gone to a great deal of work and arranged with these riders who had thrown themselves into their performance, this very real portrayal, right down to the clothing. Timing would have been a key factor in pulling it off as anything even close to authentic.

Josiah let out a deep breath and felt a little light-headed. He realized that he had been holding his breath off and on through the whole reenactment, and suddenly felt the liberty to be able to breathe normally.

"I had no idea exactly what Pete had planned," said Mr. Jack honestly. "I worked the script into it, but, to tell you the truth, Pete, I am so impressed. I hope the boys don't have nightmares tonight." He smiled at his son.

"I hope I don't have nightmares tonight," Pete said. "Man, weren't those guys great?"

Way off in the distance they could see the cloud of dust being left by the retreating riders. They wondered how far they had to go before they would be home. They would, no doubt, have quite a story to tell when they got there.

Chapter Twenty

Discharging the Guard

They set up camp a little away from the water that night. Before they retired they gathered around the fire and sang a song based on the song of deliverance and triumph in Exodus 15. Again, it was obvious that Pete had put much effort into composing the piece. It was powerful, meaningful, and alive with the spirit of what was going on.

It echoed across the land on both sides of the river, and, as before, even the coyotes joined in. Everyone could feel the force of truth behind it, as all of them had already seemed to have had their faith challenged and had come out victorious. They had taken on the enemy, Satan; actually the LORD had gone down into the crevice of his crawlspace and dragged him out, and God had proven Himself to be triumphant. Satan had been forced to back off for a season.

At that moment, if anyone in the group had been questioned, they would have answered that they would never in all their lives consider walking away from so great a God as our God, if they should live to be over one hundred. There was no call for nightmares, and nothing to be afraid of. After all, had not the LORD proven it; and wasn't that the point?

It had been an exhausting day, but there was peace and joy in the camp that night. There was no doubt that everyone would sleep well; resting under the wings of the only One Who can properly care for us. He has said it would be that way if we reflect upon His goodness.

There had been a little something more that Mr. Jack had wanted to share with the group, but decided that it was best left until morning. In no way could he improve upon what the LORD had done tonight, and he certainly did not wish to take away from it. He had learned that it wasn't enough to hold the truth and to have a Word from God for His people, but that timing was equally as important. After all, it was the word that was fitly spoken that was like apples of gold in pictures of silver. Even a good word spoken at the wrong time, can do more harm than good.

Many of the leaders including Mr. Jack's family, stayed up well into the night, full of what the LORD had done that day even in their own lives. They talked of not only this place, but about home, and life in general. They spoke of family, friends, the state of church, and of national and international affairs, for somehow that spirit had been kindled.

They spoke of the greatness of the plan of God, and, no matter how strong the person, the need for constant reminders. Tonight had certainly evidenced that truth in each of them, and, happily, they felt they would never be the same for it. In only a few days, adults and children alike had come alive in some new way. Ideas about changes and plans of things to do when they returned home were running through their minds. Mr. Jack knew that this was the stuff that true revival was made from. He was more than a little excited, for there were representatives from many areas here. This spirit, he knew was contagious.

The following morning Pete let everyone sleep later. He did not go to waken Juanito until seven o'clock. There was no need, he decided, and nothing good to be gained from it.

The four boys woke to the resonant sound of the shofar just after seven. "Hey, it's after seven o'clock," pointed out Cameron when they met outside their tents. No one had anything to add to that. They didn't seem to care. That was good.

As they went down to the river Josiah, still into the spirit of the thing said, "Hey, let's see if we can find any dead bodies."

Everyone in the group laughed but no one carried it as far as they might have under normal circumstances, for the reality of last night was still with them.

By seven-thirty everyone was seated on the bank of the river enjoying their breakfast. No one seemed to mind that it was the same food. Somehow this morning it tasted like a new menu. "Anyway," pointed out Josiah, "babies eat the same baby food or formula all the time. They don't seem to mind."

"Well," began Mr. Jack, "it seems you boys were pushed pretty heavily yesterday by our friend Pete, so we've decided to camp out another night right where we are. It looks like this place might need some exploring. What do you think?"

Everyone, including the leaders, cheered, for this was a very pleasant spot. It afforded shade and water and a variety of colors to enjoy. The boys were excited.

"There was one more thing I wanted to share, but felt that it could wait until morning," Mr. Jack continued. "In keeping with the theme of this Stopping Places adventure, I wanted to mention our friends, the Kurds.

What we saw and heard last night, having to do with the hand of God on His people Israel and against the enemy of His people, Egypt, was very powerful. But, the Kurds have not been quite so blessed. That is an understatement. Imagine a similar plight, but from a different people and a different time. The people in the wilderness are the Kurds and the enemy is none other than the ruthless Iraqi dictator, Saddam Hussein who ruled from 1979 until 2003. He was executed in 2006 for his crimes, but not before he was responsible for the deaths of hundreds of thousands of Iraqis. He was cruel and brutal, seeming to respect no limits. He was a widow-maker and left hundreds of thousands of orphans without provision or provider.

Hussein's plan was to weaken the valiant Kurds; many of them just came up amongst the missing. Of course, they were killed; many buried in mass graves; later uncovered by soldiers. Their blood still cries out from the land, even as the blood of the Jew cries out from camps like Auschwitz in Germany.

When the Kurds had their backs against the Red Sea, so-to-speak, the waters did not part for them. They truly were trapped with no place to go, with a fearsome enemy railing and following through with threats. Of course, they had not been serving God. Today, though, many of them are open to the Words of Life from God's Word. As I said earlier, God has used hands to turn the keys to open those doors, even as Christ used hands of healing to open the doors in His day that they might not only hear, but listen to the Words of Truth.

There is only one way to avenge the blood of those who have been murdered, and that is with the blood of Jesus, not vengeance as man looks upon it, but vengeance against the real enemy, Satan, who is the mastermind behind the plans and workings of evil men.

You all have a part in building homes for some of these no-longer-forgotten people, and, if you are praying for them, you have a part in building a life for them that will ripple throughout eternity. You have no idea."

Everyone was quiet as they reflected on the words that Mr. Jack had spoken as they joined hands and prayed. The day felt right and good.

"That being said, now," he continued, "before we go exploring, let's take a trip down to the river and do our laundry. It won't take long. What do you say?" Everyone went to change into shorts that they could get right into the water as they washed their clothes. Mr. Jack saw there would be no problem trying to coerce anyone to do laundry. If he didn't know any better, he would have thought they were having fun with it.

It hadn't taken long for them to get into the water. Already they were enjoying themselves. In no time lines were strung here and there between branches of the trees and laden with dripping wet clothes.

"Let's be sure we explore only north and east because tomorrow morning we will be headed south," said Mr. Jack. "We don't want to take any of the fun out of it. There are plenty of caves and caverns I saw just north of here from the other side of the river. I'm sure you guys spotted them too."

All twelve tribes left together and headed north. One small mountain peak stood away from a larger chain just northeast of it that the group felt would make great exploring.

"Maybe some bandits hid some gold up here years ago," suggested Josiah, ever looking for the thrill of adventure. "It looks like it would be a good spot with all the caves and jagged rocks. If I wanted a hiding place, I would use this one," he added.

Everyone laughed but his comments did cause the other boys to wonder if there might be some treasure in these hills. After all, through the years there had been much gold recorded as never recovered. "What if we did find gold, Mr. Jack?" asked Zachary, already calculating.

"I have the landowner's word that whatever we find of value belongs to us," he said smiling at the boys. "I like that kind of an arrangement. I wouldn't mind giving him a 'piece of the action' but somehow if we have to do all the work and then turn it all over to him, it doesn't seem like quite so much fun," he laughed.

Patty nudged him. "Oh, Jack," she said, nodding her head back and forth.

"What?" he said, acting as though he was hurt or, at least, misunderstood, "now what did I say?"

"Let's not make this about a treasure hunt," she continued. "You had your treasure hunting last summer."

"Now, Patty," he said, "I'm just responding to the boys' questions. Isn't that what I'm here for, after all? Don't begrudge me my calling. And, you wouldn't mind if God wanted to bless us with a little treasure, would you?"

"No, she answered honestly, "I guess I'd be lying if I said I would object."

The base of the little mountain was about two miles in circumference. "This is a good size for us to fan out and investigate," Mr. Jack said. "As best we can, we can spread out like the twelve numbers on the clock. We'll be number twelve, so number six will be across from us, directly through the mountain.

There must be plenty of caves and rocks to explore. Just be careful. No one strays from their group. Remember don't blow those whistles unless there's an emergency. We'll meet back at the camp between eleven and twelve, if not earlier. That gives us over three hours. This afternoon we'll probably want to hit the water. It's going to be a hot day."

Pete took up the challenge and assigned each of them a number on their imaginary clock. This was going to be fun. Somehow, Mr. Jack sensed a bit of competition again. He liked it.

The tribes broke up, half taking the east side, and half the west, and began to walk the circumference of the base to find a good spot to begin to ascend. Everyone had their canteen, whistle, flashlight, and staff. Some, like Zach, had cameras.

Siah was glad that he had left Mustgofast back at the campsite. The climb would have been too steep. Four of the women had opted to stay back at camp and cook a supply of beans. They were looking forward to a day of relaxing after yesterday's grueling pace.

There was always a big kettle of beans soaking in water with a little salt and vinegar, and every time they made camp, Randy put a kettle of beans on the fire. Sometimes they would cook all night. He had it down to a science. Beans and sourdough bread were his specialties. Though the boys knew they would be good and tired of beans before they left for home, there was no one in all the tribes that did not like them.

When Mr. Jack had commented on the goodness of Randy's cooking, Randy responded, "That's one thing that I could do better than Sylvie: cook. She was alright, but I was better." After he said that he laughed and added "I can't believe that I actually said that out loud. Until now I was not even willing to face the truth about that, as though it would be a put-down to my wife. Probably sounds like nonsense to you, huh, Jack?"

"Not at all," Jack answered honestly. "Actually, maybe we're both messed up in the head, because I can understand that."

As they began to ascend, Randy thought again of Sylvie. How she had enjoyed climbing and exploring. They never found too much that had any monetary value, but they sure did have a lot of fun and many fond memories. Until this time, he had not allowed himself the luxury of going through his mental file of those precious souvenirs. He had locked it tightly and posted a big, ugly guard outside its door, without even realizing it.

In his mind's eye, he demanded the keys from the guard, discharged him, and told him that he had already been paid too well; he needn't look for more or any kind of a favorable recommendation. He would get neither.

Chapter Twenty-one

Old Deaf Elk

In their tribe Mr. Jack and Zachary were the only ones with cameras. That was sufficient for they would share with the tribe whatever pictures were worth remembering and with those in the whole group whatever might be of interest to everyone. Already they had a nice collection of memorabilia.

"I hope we get some good shots today, Mr. Jack," said Zach, as they headed up the mountain. "I want to get some wildlife."

"Well, I'm not sure how much we'll see because of course, unless they're old and deaf, they'll hear us long before we get anywhere near them. Maybe we'll catch a few plants that aren't terrified and will actually strike up a pose for us."

Zach laughed at the image he had going through his mind of plants actually backing away and of a photo labeled, "*An Old Deaf Elk*". He'd have to remember that. It was funny.

Ahead of time the twelve tribes had agreed that they should go all the way to the top first and do their exploring on the way down. That seemed to be most logical as they would have surmised what might be worth exploring. What a shame it would be, after all, to miss something great near the top because too much time was spent on the lesser closer to the base. That made sense to everyone.

The Levites stopped to rest about half way up. The air was a little thinner and they didn't want this to turn into a marathon. "Let's stop for a drink, Mr. Jack suggested, "Besides, these old muscles need a bit of a rest. It's been a while since they've had a work-out like this. How 'bout you, Patty?"

Mrs. Patty quickly agreed. "For your sake we best stop a while, Jack," she smiled back. That didn't get past anyone; they knew she needed rest too.

Already they could see a view of the campsite. Though there were trees, they were sparse, and they were sitting on the edge of one of the rock ledges that jutted out. They could see for miles; the sky looked so big from up here.

Zach took some video footage, but realized something of the view would be lost as the camera could not accurately portray the whole panoramic view. But for anyone up here viewing it, he was sure the video would bring it back into their minds.

The sky was clear and a soft blue with only a few fluffy clouds. Four birds with wide wing spans circled high above. The boys imagined them to be eagles, but there was no saying for sure, as they were too high.

"Those birds are probably wondering why all the shepherds are headed for the top of the mountain," said Josiah. "Even though they are high up, I'm sure they know we are here and they have already spotted our shepherd's staffs.

I was hoping to see a few animals, but I don't think anything but squirrels and birds live up here. We haven't seen any tracks or other signs of animals. I've been looking for them."

"Well, this area;" pointed out Randy, "let's call it the twelfth longitude, is pretty steep and stony. If there are animals, they would use a gentler slope and a little easier under the feet, don't you think?"

That made sense to Josiah as he quickly picked up again on the hope of seeing an animal or two before they returned to camp.

They had not much distance to reach the top when Randy said, "I doubt whether we'll see any animals from here on up because there really isn't much for them up here. Notice how sparse the vegetation is?"

No sooner had he gotten that out of his mouth than Juanito pointed up the hill. Coming down were three sheep. "Look," whispered Zach with his camera already in motion.

"Bighorn sheep," said Randy, as though he were a tour guide for the group. Guess I was wrong; so much for my observations," he smiled.

The sheep continued downhill at a reasonably fast pace, as though they were in a panic.

"Something must have scared them," said Brian. "They came pretty close, Zach. I hope you got some good footage."

"I'm sure he did," answered Josiah. "He's good with that camera. Man, I can't believe I saw some bighorn sheep."

"Well, we're not likely to see many more animals going the last quarter distance," said Randy. "Of that I'm pretty sure."

Moments later, not seventy feet from where they spotted the sheep, they heard a running sound just to the right of them.

"Shh!" said Juanito, really into the wildlife thing now himself.

They all stood as still as statues. From above came a sizeable black bear with her cub, lumbering down the hill. She too seemed to be hurrying her little one along as though moving away from danger.

"Wow!" said Randy. "I don't get it. Where'd they come from? They don't normally go that high into the mountains. They prefer to stay where there are caves, water, and trees or at least some brush-cover."

From the peak a voice echoed down. It was one of the boys from another tribe. "Hello Levites. Are you coming?"

The Levites line of travel, that is the twelfth meridian, had turned out to be the steepest, and so, of course, took the longest to climb.

"Of course!" shouted Randy. "I get it! With the tribes closing in on them from around the mountain the animals moved to higher ground. The closer they got to the top, the closer the tribes were. We formed a drive; a human network around them, surrounding them. Because we're probably the furthest from the top, we are the weakest place in the net and the only hope for the animals. If we're quiet, we may even see more. Let's lay low for a time. All the noise on the top of the hill is even more apt to chase whatever animals there are past us. We couldn't have planned it any better."

Sure enough, in no time a lone gray wolf raced past them heading straight down the mountain.

"I think he lost his brakes," whispered Josiah. "Man, isn't this great?"

After more yelling and noise from above, the group decided that there would probably be no more wildlife. They were certain that more must have headed down the mountain before the net had closed; walking or running right past them. Josiah wished that they had figured out what was happening before they were so close to the peak so they could have been on the lookout for them. Still, he sure was happy at what they had seen and with the fact that Zach had missed none of it with his camera. The animals had not been the only ones surprised.

No one of all the other eleven tribes had seen so much as one animal.

"We shot all the trophies," said Zach, holding up his camera victoriously.

"Sometimes it pays to be the last one to the top," said Christopher, matter-of-factly. Everyone waited to see what else he had to say about it, but he offered nothing more. He felt, I guess, that the facts spoke for themselves. Those who came in last, in this case anyway, had gotten the consolation prize.

"I guess what counts," said Mrs. Patty, "is that we all tried our best, and we all made it. The view from the top is offered to all of us and it is gorgeous!" There certainly was no denying that.

After spending ten minutes on the peak together they were ready to head down and do a little exploring. They had about an hour-and-a-half before they had to be back in camp. They had seen some caves worth visiting.

As they headed down Mr. Jack poked Zachary and said, "That sure was better than an old deaf elk, my friend. Goes to show you how much I know." Both of them had a good laugh.

Chapter Twenty-two

Everyone Has a Story

Walking down the mountain they spotted several different varieties of birds. Though they must have certainly been there as they walked up, their minds had been so engrossed in spotting four-legged animals that they seemed to have missed the winged ones, other than those circling high above.

For a time they stopped to film a beautiful western bluebird. His deep purplish-blue throat and rusty-orange breast as he perched upon a low branch, cocking his head from one side to the other, made him look almost plastic against the perfect background of greens.

Once he sounded a soft, short warble, by which they all knew that he was showing off. Even Randy said it, and, of course, that made it official.

Mr. Jack noted how great Randy interacted with the boys and wondered if he had children of his own. He figured he had none, for it seemed he would have mentioned them as he was talking about his wife.

"Say, Randy," said Mr. Jack. "Did you and Sylvia ever have any children? You're so good with them."

"Sylvie is buried beside our only son. He was three years old when he died from an allergic reaction to bees. We never knew he had it. He had been stung once before and seemed to fare well, though, of course he cried. The doctor said that the venom from the first sting was stored in his bloodstream, his body not able to rid itself of the poison, and the second sting, though a year later, put him over the edge.

It all happened so quickly. We were on our way to the hospital when the LORD called him home right in Sylvie's arms.

I think she handled it better than I did. She mourned but she would say as much to herself as to me, 'Honey, the LORD knows what He is doing. It is difficult but you know that one day we will see Richie again.'

She would cry softly in my arms, and I would cry even more and longer, and together we would fall asleep that way.

Richie was the handsomest little dickens you ever did see. He was bright and personable, happy and easy to manage. He wanted to go everywhere I went. He just loved life on the ranch. He would sit up on my horse holding the saddle horn right in front of me. He would sit with me on the tractor. He liked the tractors, but, man, he loved the horses. He would be fourteen years old now.

For whatever reason, we just never had any more children. I can almost hear Sylvie's voice telling me that it simply wasn't God's plan. Though it is not always easy to accept, I know she was right.

I'll tell you, my friend," he said pensively, "losing a three-year-old is just something you're never prepared for. You know?" The boys in the tribe all heard what Randy had said for when he began to speak they all became quiet. They were all thinking of the son who would be around their age and trying to picture him.

"I can only imagine how difficult it was for you," stated Mr. Jack simply. There was no reason to add any more to it, for Randy knew he meant it.

"Sylvie," Randy continued, as though thinking out loud, "was taken away almost as suddenly. She had gotten that flu that was going around five or so years ago, and thought nothing of it. She was rarely sick, exceptionally strong, ate right, and had no health issues at all. She seemed much younger than her years.

When she wasn't getting better, I told her she needed to go to the clinic. At first she balked up, but I kept on her about it.

Finally, after about four or five days of a fever, I told her she was going whether she liked it or not. 'I don't feel like losing my wife over this flu. People have died from it, Sylvie,' I said.

She laughed at me and said something like, 'Oh, Randy, you are so dramatic. If it will make you feel better, I'll go to the clinic.'

They listened to her lungs and had me take her to the nearby hospital. She had double pneumonia. I stayed with her, of course, and she went to be with the LORD at exactly 3:00 AM the following morning.

She had gone to sleep when we got to the hospital. She kissed me good-night and smiled, telling me not to worry, but to trust in the LORD.

Just before three she opened her eyes. 'Randy,' she said, 'I'm going home now. Richie and I will be there when you get there. You'll be fine.' She closed her eyes and simply went back to sleep. Five minutes later she drew her last breathe, just as peacefully as can be, and, even as she said, she went home."

There was a comfortable pause as everyone reflected on his words. It was sad for Randy, of course, but he had told the story so gloriously that no one felt sorry for Sylvia.

"And, here I have been, over five years later; still in Limbo. I'm glad Sylvie couldn't see me, or, for sure, there would have been sadness in heaven. But, thanks to this trip; no more. I have cried buckets of tears, but regarding my wife and son, I shall cry no more in sadness. I thank God for His patience with me."

"Hey," said Cameron, "isn't that the cave we were going to explore?"

"It sure is," smiled Randy. Though the boys liked him before hearing his story, they all saw him through new eyes now. Meme' was right when she said that everyone has a story. Sometimes the greatest therapy we can offer is just to listen and allow them to tell it.

The ledge that made up the roof of the cave jutted high above the land, jagged and rocky. They walked down and around to where they could gain access to the entrance.

"I hope there are no animals hibernating in there," said Josiah, his imagination now going wild with him.

"No," Randy responded, "the animals that hibernate have all been awake now for a few months. They hibernate through the winter. That is not to say that this might not be a type of home for some though. We'll make a little noise before entering, just to be certain we don't disturb an animal who is taking a midday nap. It might not do to waken him.

"Look!" shouted Brian. "What is it?"

"Back away and give her some room," said Randy. "We've disturbed her time with her kittens. It's a female lynx. See the tufts coming up from her ears. Isn't she a beauty? Up until a few years ago they had almost disappeared from Colorado, but they were reintroduced and have had a comeback.

Look at her with her young. They're about two months old. She looks to weigh about twenty-five pounds, and just look at the size of those rear feet. They can walk right across the snow as though they're wearing snowshoes and bound like a rabbit.

They are silent, ferocious, and swift hunters. I wouldn't want to mess with an angry mama. Let's back away and find another cave to explore. There was one further down."

Zach zoomed in with his camera to get a close-up of the magnificent cat. She was alert as though waiting for their next move. She didn't appear to be concerned that she was outnumbered. Who knew; maybe she could sense or even smell fear, or, for that matter, that they meant her no harm. In any event, they backed away.

One-third of a mile down the way they came to another cave. They had only spotted two coming up. Even if this one held no adventure, they felt they had had their share for the morning. They had been left with much to write in their journals already.

This time they made a little more noise before they approached the mouth of the cave. They didn't want to surprise a more ferocious animal; perhaps a bear with her cubs. They didn't need that kind of adventure.

The cave did not extend far back. They used their flashlights looking to discover something in the crevices and nooks, but, it seemed, man and animal had been disinterested in this one. They were not sorry though, for their stomachs were making every effort to coax them back to camp.

As they headed downhill again Josiah said, "Man, I'm sure my stomach has probably scared the rest of the animals away from the twelfth meridian. It's growling like a ferocious beast."

Randy liked Josiah.

Chapter Twenty-three

The Wilderness of Shur

The ladies had the meal all prepared when they arrived back in the camp. It was not quite noon. As they supposed, the Levites were the first tribe to arrive. Traveling along the steepest meridian had its advantages; in particular, coming down. That same slope which had slowed them so much on the way up helped persuade them to move right along.

Several of the other tribes came in not far behind them. When all had arrived in the camp they discovered that aside from birds, squirrels, and chipmunks, the rest had seen no other wildlife.

"Of course you wouldn't have. The animals that went past us as we walked up," said Randy unsympathetically toward the other tribes, "are probably still on the run. If that's their home they've probably decided that it was time to move anyway. 'After all', they're probably saying to each other, 'yesterday a whole group of noisy humans walked by coming down from the North on the other side of the river.

Then they made camp too close for comfort. And if that weren't enough, last night another bunch came in from the East. When they arrived there was much screaming and yelling from both groups. Then they crossed the river. I mean, who knew what was going on anyway? The whole thing was very confusing.

Finally, the second group left, leaving the first who had moved their camp to our side of the river. Then, this morning, they all surrounded us and climbed the mountain. The only weapons they had were sticks that each of them were carrying. And, if they hadn't been so out of breath, they might have beaten us with them.

Man, we're out of here! People really are the strangest animals. You just never know what they'll do. I mean, what's next?'" Everyone laughed at his long imaginary account of the animals' take of the recent events.

After lunch they swam for the afternoon. The whole group was relaxed and had a wonderful time. Some of them did more exploring upstream, but it seemed almost anticlimactic after yesterday's activities. The truth was that as the day progressed they began looking forward to tomorrow when they would be traveling again.

After supper they sat around and sang and told stories. Especially interesting were those Mr. Jack had to tell of his ventures when he was young and some of those of the Mideast. He sure was a great story-teller.

They turned in early by choice, as they discovered that they were tired again, even though they hadn't kept up the grueling pace of yesterday.

Every night when the music began, the boys agreed, it was like something of a lullaby spirit gripped them, and they could barely keep their eyes open. It seemed mysterious to them as they didn't feel that tired before the music.

"See you tomorrow," said Cameron, rising to head for the tent. That was all the other three needed to follow suit, as they headed out as well. "Today sure was a good day, Mr. Jack," said Josiah, as he bid them all goodnight. "We got to see the mountain and all those wild animals."

"It sure was, Siah," said Mr. Jack affectionately.

"But tomorrow's going to be even better," threw back Josiah. "I just know it."

After breakfast the next day, they packed up to head southwest, a little away from the water. "Today we are going to head for the fourth of the stopping places. We have a ways to go. We won't make it there tonight," said Mr. Jack.

"The Jews actually traveled three days into the Wilderness of Shur. We will get there, hopefully, at least according to Pete, by late tomorrow afternoon.

There is no need to race, but we are going to imagine there is a bit of an urgency because, like the Israelites, after we leave this place our water supply begins to run low and that it is actually three days' journey, rather than two. We will fill our canteens from this clear cold mountain water before we leave, and do our best to conserve. Obviously, we don't want anybody to be dehydrated, but, for the sake of authenticity, let's say that there's no place to fill the canteens for three days.

And, imagine that we traveled all day yesterday into this wilderness, instead of climbing that mountain and swimming in the afternoon as we did. Now, this would have been immediately after the Egyptians had been left dead as the waters of the Red Sea closed in upon them.

The people were not used to such a pace. Though they had been made to work hard in Egypt, this, you see, was very different. This would have been only the fourth day. Remember, the first night they spent in Succoth, the second in Etham, the third in PiHahiroth.

The next place with significance would have been after traveling three days into the Wilderness of Shur. So let us head out and see what might be waiting for us there. Keep in mind as we go that they didn't have a map. They were following the cloud by day and the fire by night. They didn't know where their next stopping place would be."

Together they prayed again with hands joined. They were all eager to see what lie ahead for them in an area they had not yet investigated.

"We're actually traveling south, southwest," said Chris. Most of the boys who heard him were dumbfounded that he seemed to know that, just from observing the sun. Of course it was directly east, and early in the morning. But the fact that he could tell so precisely was more than impressive.

"Wow," said Randy, "That's pretty good, Chris."

"Yah," said Josiah, "and I'll bet Meme' would be impressed too, Chris. And, you're right."

"And, you know that he's right, Josiah?" asked Brian. "And how old are you? Man, I don't even know much about that stuff."

The boys had to admit that they felt pretty good about themselves in knowing. Not only that, but much about geography and map-reading had stuck with them. They had really been made to study it, but, truth be known, they actually enjoyed it, though, of course, they wouldn't have told Meme' that.

For a while they had the river in sight, but eventually moved away from it, as it seemed to head directly south. They could still tell where it was, but they couldn't see the water at all.

They stopped traveling around four in the afternoon. Pete told them that it wouldn't be necessary to travel longer to be able to stop around the same time tomorrow. That would give them time to explore and just hang out a little that night. They were looking forward to stopping. No one would complain about it.

"Remember," Mr. Jack told them just before they turned in that night, "the Wilderness of Shur was not an official stopping place. They traveled through it on their way to the next stopping place. Interestingly, or at least I think so, the name Shur literally means *to travel about like a merchant and just survey and observe.* The significance is more of one passing through than looking to stay or put down roots at all.

Because we are not looking to put down roots here and because we are leaving early tomorrow, we should all turn in at a reasonable hour tonight for a good night's rest. What do you say, guys?"

No one disagreed with him, aloud or inside of themselves. He was right.

After eating, sitting around the fire, and singing and listening to Pete and Brian on their guitars they called it a night. My goodness, Josiah thought, it was amazing how tired all the fresh air and walking seemed to make him. He couldn't get over it.

Chapter Twenty-four

Sweet Bitterness

True to their plans, the following morning they were back on the trail at seven-thirty.

Mustgofast was raring to go. Josiah was wishing he could jump on his back and go for a ride, but, of course he couldn't. Though he didn't need to he held the lead rope loosely, for Mustgofast needed no persuasion to follow his boy. The last couple of days he had stayed even closer to him it seemed, lest Josiah should get any more bright ideas of exploring and leaving him behind.

Every time they stopped along the way, Josiah petted or brushed him and gave him some one-on-one attention. They 'conversed,' as was their manner.

Earlier than anticipated someone called out that they spotted a sign and took off running. The tall, lean, eighteen-year old boy from the tribe of Naphtali sprinted across the plain, covering the distance quickly.

"Mr. Jack!" he shouted. "The sign says, **Marah**! Hey, doesn't that mean *'bitter'* like in the book of Ruth? When Naomi returned from Moab with her daughter-in-law, Ruth, didn't she tell the people not to call her Naomi any more, but to call her Mara, for she was bitter? Does it mean the same?"

"Well," said Mr. Jack as he approached the sign, "you've stolen my thunder on this one here, Stephen. You are right," he said as he handed Stephen the journeyman's cards to give out to everyone.

"Let me have your canteens," Pete whispered to Juanito and Josiah, who had become close buddies. Quickly they handed their nearly empty canteens over to him as he headed for the water with theirs and his own canteen.

Mr. Jack continued, "It seems our friend Pete must be thirsty. He must not have rationed his water the way he should have and come up short. I'll wait for him to get back before I give you the rundown on this spot."

"Sorry," Pete said as he rejoined the group, though he really didn't look to be too sorry. "That's some crystal, cold water," he whispered to the two who were taking the lid off their canteens. "Let's give it a try," he said as he put his canteen to his mouth.

The boys gulped a good mouthful of it and dramatically spat it out upon the ground. "Ugh!" said Juanito.

"Something's wrong with this water," said Josiah. "It tastes nasty!"

Now Mr. Jack realized what Pete must have done again, for the sake of authenticity you understand.

He picked up his cue quickly. "Of course it's nasty," he said, as he winked at Pete who had obviously not drunk any of his. "These are bitter waters. The Bible says that when they came to this place they had not found water for three days, only to discover that they could not drink the waters here, for they were too bitter.

Then, the people began to murmur against Moses again, as though this were his fault; asking him what they were supposed to drink. Already they must have forgotten God's magnificent provision of the parting of The Red Sea. Imagine Moses' frustration? How do you babysit for two to three million people? Keep in mind that he was here because God told him to come.

After we give our hearts to the LORD, we begin to follow His path for our lives. If we stay on that path, there will be things that don't always make sense to us, such as the LORD seeming to trap us with the enemy on one side and the sea on the other. But, it is for us to immediately turn to Him; after all; He is doing the leading and we call ourselves His followers.

At this time I, that is, Moses cried out to the LORD; after all, you know, they were His people." Mr. Jack dramatically lifted his rod toward heaven and called out, "Help me LORD with these, Your people!

The LORD has heard me and spoken to me," he said, "about that tree over there."

Just a short distance from the sign was a tree which was about fifteen feet tall, with thin willowy branches. "Pete," said Mr. Jack to his son, "would you get me a hatchet from the wagon?"

Josiah and Juanito were still trying to get the bitter taste from their mouths. "Want a drink of my water?" Zach asked. Quickly Josiah took him up on it, and then handed it to Juanito, who finished what was left in the canteen.

Pete smiled at both boys and whispered, "Don't forget; you're in the leadership team and have to foot part of the responsibility that goes with it. And, remember; no grumbling or complaining." They had to smile at him in spite of the horrible taste in their mouths.

Mr. Jack walked over to the tree. "The LORD has told me to take this tree and put it into the river and the water will become sweet," he said. And so he did.

"Now," said Pete to Josiah and Juanito, "you fellas bring your canteens over here. We'll refill them and give you the first drink." He rinsed them out in the brook, refilled them, and handed them back to the two boys.

They didn't hesitate to drink from them, for they trusted that Pete had put something in their first water from his own canteen to make it taste bad. They were right. The water was fresh, cold, and refreshing, and they drank their fill. The others gathered around to fill their canteens as well. Again, Pete had gone to a great deal to make this place appear authentic.

"What was that anyway?" asked Josiah. "It tasted like something my mother cleans with."

"It was apple cider vinegar," answered Pete. "It's a little bitter, but you know I wouldn't give you anything that would harm you."

"Let's not miss the lesson here," continued Mr. Jack. "Where God leads, He prepares the way. First of all when we are in trouble though, He insists we cry out to Him, even as I did. So many times He uses what is already there as a cure for the problem.

These waters were bitter, not like the river of life at all, but God transformed them into sweet waters. He used, if you will, The Tree of Life, Who, of course is Jesus Himself, to transform them and work His miracle.

All the LORD requires is our hearts bent toward Him and our obedience. It is not difficult to understand. He will take the worst circumstance and turn something around. It is not important that we can figure out how

He's going to do it. Ours it to do what is necessary and then to stand upon God's Word. I say this not because I always do the perfect thing or make all the right choices, but, because it is true. God is just looking for a people who will totally trust Him all the time.

When things come into our lives, that seem to be as bitter pills to swallow, if we remember to ask the LORD to somehow sweeten the water, He is willing and able to do just that. It is our heritage as we travel the wilderness as pilgrims and strangers. He loves it when we trust in Him. He does not simply take the bitterness away, but actually sweetens the water."

Randy was quiet as he listened to his friend speaking. It seemed to him he may as well have been the only one there, for every word, he knew, was direct from the throne, and just for him. He had finally allowed himself to come into a position to not only hear, but listen to what the LORD had to say to him. He wondered how much more he had missed in these past five or so years.

Actually, these things were probably missed before that time, for what he knew had not sustained him during his times of trials. Perhaps he had heard them and thought he understood, but, when put to the test it seemed he understood very little.

He came to the conclusion then, that what he knew was simply not enough. The LORD had proven Himself to be faithful and patient again. Obviously he had missed something, and it had been something very important.

To this point, he had been like the Israelites with their backs to the Red Sea and their enemy closing in on them, and hadn't even recognized it. He was right there with them at Marah, complaining about the circumstances that had brought him there, instead of looking to the LORD for the answer.

It was no wonder he had felt so little blessing in his life. The LORD had, no doubt, been withholding blessing to gain his attention.

His testimony had not been a good one. Without even realizing it, he had been complaining within his heart, though his mouth would have said another thing. Like the Israelites, he had seen his life as one big sacrifice.

There were going to be some changes for him from now on. He meant to glorify God, and, as long as there was breath in his body, he would do it!

"Thank you for this Tree of Life, LORD," he said.

Everyone answered a loud, "Amen!"

Chapter Twenty-five

In His Time

That night seated around the fire, Mr. Jack spoke more of this place called Marah. "Here," he said, "is where God told His people that if they would dare to be different, a people set apart, He would ever care for them, even as He already had shown them.

God has not changed. He said that if they, and we, for that matter, would listen and obey His voice, hear and apply His Word to our lives, and do what is right, He would put none of the diseases that came upon Egypt on us, for He is the LORD that heals us.

Mr. Jack shared parts of his life and many of the things that had happened from his own testimony that the enemy had tried to use to bring bitterness into his life, and how the LORD had sweetened the water.

What a great night it was as the 'family' enjoyed their meal, sang, and talked well into the night. Mustgofast cropped the tender grass near the water's edge, not straying far from his boy.

One of the boys from the Kansas City church played a solo on his harmonica that was beautiful. No one sang with the music, but the melody didn't need lyrics. It was as though the harmonica itself was singing.

The boy who played was not much older than Josiah. Everyone marveled at what mastery he had of the instrument, and couldn't imagine how good he would play in later years. It was as though the music was preaching a message, touching the deepest part of them.

Needless to say, that night when they made their way to their beds, all was well in their world; with everyone, I mean; not just the four boys.

"In one way," Josiah said to Zach before they went to sleep, "this trip is nowhere near as adventurous as last year's, but, in another, it's been even better. Know what I mean, Zach?"

"I sure do, Siah. I love it," he whispered.

The following morning they headed out again a little after eight. There didn't seem to be any hurry. They had gotten into a routine of sorts and knew how to read Pete's body language and to follow his prompting.

"Tomorrow," Mr. Jack said, as they began walking, "we should be able to do a little laundry again, or maybe even this afternoon, if it's not too late when we reach the next spot. What do you think, Pete?"

"That should work out," Pete replied, though he gave no indicator if it would be this afternoon or the following day.

"Perhaps we'll stay a few days at the next spot," said Pete as they sat down for lunch. "How would that be with everybody?"

A loud "Hurrah!" went up from the crowd.

"Will there be water there?" one of the boys from another tribe dared to ask.

"For sure," answered Pete, "or we couldn't stay."

Now in the minds of the boys, that meant that there would probably be a good amount of it. That also meant that there might be some exploring in the area.

Just before two that afternoon Josiah, for so he had made up his mind to do it this time, spotted the next stopping place sign. He didn't say a word, but took off running before anyone else knew what had happened. Mustgofast, of course, was there right beside him.

The other Levites, but for the adults, ran behind as well. "The sign says **Elim**, Mr. Jack," shouted back Josiah, "and it's not even two o'clock yet!" The adults laughed at the excitement in his voice. "Look, just over that little hill, it looks like another river!"

Everyone could see why Pete had mentioned that they might stay in this spot for a few days. It was gorgeous. It looked like an advertisement for a fine vacation resort. They had gone from a brownish plain in the morning, to a green meadow whose southwest edge was lined with beautiful trees, though not densely wooded. The trees looked as though they had been carefully planted years ago by a master gardener, (and, indeed they had) and ran all the way to the knoll, almost to the water's edge. The sign had been placed halfway between the water and the meadow.

"I have never seen a more beautiful spot," said Mrs. Patty. "It fairly takes the breath away."

"Wait 'til you check out the river, Ma," said Pete, pleased that she seemed so taken by this place. He had thought when he found this place that her reaction would be like this, for he knew his mother quite well.

"Jack," she went on, as though they might have been there alone, "can't you just picture a little log cabin with some lovely flowers and a nice vegetable garden a little closer to the water? Imagine the wildlife we would see. This is what dreams are made of."

"Forget it, Patty," Mr. Jack smiled. "It isn't going to happen," he said, rolling his eyes toward heaven for the sake of everyone watching. "Don't even dream about it."

"Now, Jack," she said, smiling. "It isn't like you to stifle anyone's dreams. Aren't you the one who preaches all the time that the church doesn't dream big enough? You can't accuse me of not listening."

"Por favor?" said Juanito, looking for his translator so he might ask a question.

"He wants to know if we can run over and check out the water?" quickly interpreted Josiah. "That's the same thing I was going to ask."

"Sure," said Mr. Jack. "We'll decide where we'll camp in a little while. Let's go check it out."

Siah and Juanito were the first two there, with Mustgofast, of course. The brook flowed from the hills. In some spots it formed pools that looked deep enough to actually dive into and swim freely, while in others the water was shallow enough to cross easily.

"This looks like a good spot to pan for gold, Mr. Jack!" shouted Josiah. "Look, the water comes from that mountain range over there," he said, pointing northwest.

The whole group of tribes had come alive; revived by the beauty of this spot and Josiah's enthusiasm.

"Let's go back and set up camp so we can go do some looking around," suggested Randy, who seemed as excited as the boys. "This place is begging to be explored."

Back amongst the trees they went, where they had left their gear. "You can set up right here or even a little closer to the water, since the trees run almost to it. Just be sure you have their cover. It looks like it's going to be a hot one today. We don't want to be out in the open.

I'd say Pete outdid himself again. What a great scout he turned out to be."

"I can't take all the credit," he responded modestly. "Though my brother Josh couldn't be with us, he explored the land with me," he said loudly enough so everyone could hear. "We had such a great time together. Just the two of us have never done anything like that. We camped out for almost a week. We rode on horseback across the land. Man, this landowner has thousands of acres. What a beautiful spread the LORD has prepared for him."

"And, for us!" added Josiah; not because he didn't want to be left out, but rather in the way he had of acknowledging God's personal touch in his life. He really felt that everything beautiful in his life, the LORD had put there especially for his enjoyment. Again, Mr. Jack thought how great it would be if we, as adults, would do the same.

After they set up, Mr. Jack asked Josiah to get the journeyman's cards from behind the sign and hand them out. Everyone was sitting down and looking very excited.

Before Mr. Jack began his eyes scanned the crowd. Everyone was quiet. He noticed how that in such a few days, actually, about a week, everyone seemed to have changed considerably. They really were like family. The adults looked healthy and at peace with the world. Everyone's color was great, and no one complained about the food, as far as he knew.

His own body which had ached much at the start from the new challenge, felt healthier. Already he could walk more briskly and for longer periods of time without tiring. It really was quite remarkable, he thought.

"How is everybody?" he asked generally. "Are you having a pretty good time?"

Everyone responded loudly and with a cheer for Mr. Jack.

"Have you made some new friends?" he continued.

Again everyone cheered.

"Isn't this great?" he asked, as though requesting a personal response of each individual. "At the risk of sounding corny, can't you just tell that it is God's appointment for us for this hour?"

Humbled by the spirit of the question everyone answered, but a little quieter this time, as most reflected on the fact that the Creator should care so much to set this whole thing up.

There is no doubt about it. God is good!

Chapter Twenty-six

The Watchmen

"This place called Elim," Mr. Jack began, "was on the edge of the Wilderness of Sin (pronounced 'seen'). The name **Elim** is significant of strength and might, like an oak tree. It was here that the Israelites found seventy strong palm trees. Today, by the way, that spot has increased to over two thousand palm trees. There were twelve wells there, probably one for each of the twelve tribes of Israel.

This was like an oasis in the desert. How wonderful it must have seemed to them. Just think that if we find this place beautiful, we who have not been oppressed by the Egyptians for so many years, how welcome this spot must have been."

"Some of us have been oppressed," said Randy.

Mr. Jack waited to see if he would say more, but, apparently, he had been thinking out loud again. "But, you see, for us it is very similar, for we had, in a sense, been living in Egypt until we gave our lives to the LORD.

When we came to Him we were blessed by divine deliverance. Next, he showed us His covering and guidance, and then His hand of protection, as Satan tries to lure us back or even to kill us.

Still not done, after the LORD Himself deals with the enemy, He convinces us that the waters of bitterness cannot sustain this new life in us. We must let go, and the only way we can is through Him, that is, the Blood of Jesus, the Tree of Life.

And, as we continue to walk in His way, He draws us to this oasis, of sorts; a most beautiful place; greater than anything we have ever seen. While it is a spiritual resort, if you will, a stopping place along the way, it is not a retirement home. For the Christian, the retirement home has a name; it is Heaven.

There will never be a time in this life where we can retire from the attacks of the enemy or the demands of life, though they may change as we get older, but, thank God for an occasional oasis where we may regroup and gather our strength back. For many that is every day in their prayer closets.

It is written in the Word that our eyes have not seen, nor have we heard, nor can the heart even comprehend the full extent of the beauty of the things that God has prepared for those who love Him. That, my friends, is speaking of before we go to heaven; those things that He has for us in this life.

Yes, there are and will continue to be many trials, tribulations, and difficult times in this life, but, the LORD has set up 'hospitals' along the way. They are beautiful, such as this place; like an oasis in the desert. But the even greater thing is that we don't necessarily have to leave our homes to get to them. Thank God!"

Most shouted, "Amen!" at this point.

Mr. Jack continued, "The Bible tells us that the Israelites camped at Elim for a time. Remember, it was on the edge of the Wilderness of Sin, which is a desert place.

When they left Elim, they had been gone for one month to the day. And so we, like them, shall stay awhile. Now, who's ready to get into that water and do some laundry?"

Everyone jumped to their feet to run in and get their dirty clothes, change into shorts, and head for the water. It was a hot afternoon, though the breezes in this area cooled it off considerably. Even the adults couldn't wait to get into the stream.

The temperature of the water was perfect. It was a bit cool from its mountainous origin not far off in the distance, and very refreshing.

The landscape was a busy one in that it seemed to afford about everything a group of boys might view as pleasant to the eyes. There were huge rock ledges to climb close by, which also held promises of caves. There were mountains, green meadows, beautiful trees, and of course, there was a playground of water.

As they were doing there laundry the boys noticed trails on both sides of the river made, no doubt, by animals of different sizes and sorts coming to drink.

They were excited, for they surmised that if they were quiet, even as Randy had suggested, close to dusk, around the time that the sun set, they might get to see some of them coming to drink.

Mr. Jack heard them talking about it and quickly volunteered to announce, as soon as they sat down to eat, that everyone must stay with their tribe and be quiet for at least an hour at dusk. They might spot some animals to mark in their journals. "It will be hard to mask the fact that one hundred, forty-six people are camping here, but you never know," he said.

"It could happen," said Josiah.

Since the plan was for them to stay in this spot for more than one day, the boys opted to save their exploring until tomorrow. They all agreed that playing in the water was the order of the day, in fact, even with doing only that, the rest of the afternoon passed quickly.

In no time they were sitting down to supper; looking forward to the night watch. "Let's imagine the animals to be enemy troops from the Old Testament time," began Pete, after they finished eating.

"These troops think they'll sneak up on us in the camp, but we are watchmen and plan on missing nothing. We have decided that we will spot them before they can do any damage to us. That's our job; it's what watchmen do."

Everyone was thrilled by Pete's tone, and at how much he seemed 'into' this whole adventure. It wasn't only the Levites who had talked much about Pete and how different this trip might have been without him. He didn't see himself as anything special, but all the boys felt - no, not just the boys; the adults as well – that this time would not have played out the same without him. There was no doubt that God could have used someone else to do what Pete was doing, but, everyone was glad it was Pete.

"Now remember," he continued, "we are not armed with earthly weapons. We can't shoot the enemy; we must spot him first and then plan our attack to defeat him in our lives. So then, first, ours is to recognize who and where the enemy is, then to deal with him however we must, so he won't make it into our camp."

They sang together after they finished eating and cleaning up, and then listened to Mr. Jack tell of some of his adventures in other lands. The beauty of it was that he was not telling stories he made up, but recounting things that were real. Even the adults were captivated as again, his stories took them to places that most of them would otherwise never be able to visit. It was great and helped to pass the time until dusk for the boys who were all keyed-up for their adventure as watchmen.

Long before the appointed time the twelve tribes had gathered in what they felt were strategic points of viewing for them; hidden from the animals. The leaders sat with their groups and all talked quietly together, sharing testimonies of their own lives, spontaneously.

Finally, the agreed upon hour came and everyone became quiet. By now, even the most rambunctious of the boys had become used to following the direction of their leaders. They had heard much of the importance of team cooperation and its necessity. Absolutely no one balked up. Everyone drew silent and the only words were those whispered to the tribes by their leaders.

Though quiet on the outside, Josiah was anything but quiet on the inside. Butterflies were playing tag in his stomach from the anticipation of what he might see.

Fifteen minutes later, (by the way; a long time for an energetic hard-to-sit-still boy like Josiah) they spotted a deer, cautiously making her way to the water. She looked behind, and they all thought she must have certainly smelled them. She turned partially around and, from the edge of the woods, came her gangly fawn.

The whole scene took Josiah's breath away. He was not alone. He had seen many deer in his life, for he lived in the country. For boys like Roberto and Juanito however, who lived in the city, this was a rare, if ever, viewing of wildlife that wasn't behind fences, concrete walls, or bars.

Cautiously the doe approached the water with her fawn, and the two drank their fill. Though she hadn't picked up on the presence of her many viewers, she was alert and watchful. For all they knew, she had never seen a human being, but was on the lookout for any animal wanting to make a quick meal of her fawn.

Quickly the deer headed back to the deeper woods where they would have more shelter. Zachary's camera had been running from the time the animals had come into view. He was more than thrilled by what he imagined the video must look like.

Pete whispered to the group after the deer left. "Well, there goes the enemy. We watched them right out of the place and they never came into the camp, Glory to God."

Now everyone had to admit that there was no way they had even thought to view the deer as enemies. If this was really true and those had been enemies, the whole group, including Pete, would have been fooled, mesmerized by the beauty of their appearance.

Ten minutes later a pack of six wolves, including two youngsters, made their way to the water. They were much bolder than the deer had been, unconcerned, or so it appeared, about any danger that might be lurking in the shadows. They visited the same spot from which the deer had just drunk and were sniffing the ground with their ears perked up.

When they finished drinking the one who appeared to be the leader lifted his nose into the air and hurriedly made his way, not forward or from where they had just come, but in the direction the deer had taken into the woods.

Josiah knew they weren't supposed to talk, but he wanted to ask if it was a waste of time to pray for an animal. Anyway, he had already done it. He had prayed that the deer and her fawn would escape being found by the pack of wolves. He knew that the wolves had to eat too, but somehow he couldn't handle the possibility that maybe the deer were today's menu.

Just then Pete interrupted his thoughts by voicing part of what was running through his mind. "It's a little easier to view the wolf as an enemy," he whispered. "Especially as he heads off in the direction the deer went not ten minutes ago."

He continued to whisper, "Keep in mind this is the life of these animals. This happens all the time and is part of nature and of God's plan for them. Animals were actually put here by God for man. It is so easy to put them in a place they don't belong. That is not to say we shouldn't take care of them as best we can. We are certainly not to be cruel to any animal, but, the fact remains, they are beasts, not human beings. We must be careful not to cross that line by viewing them as something they are not. It's not hard to do that because our domesticated animals in particular have personalities that endear us to them. Look, for example, at Josiah with Mustgofast. They make a very timely illustration of the bond that can happen between man and animal."

They returned to their viewing. They were almost ready to go back to the camp when a bull elk showed up on the scene. He was huge and appeared unconcerned about possible danger. He meandered into the water, drank his fill, and then crossed over to the other side. From there he walked toward the meadow that the group had first come into Elim from.

After some time of seeing no more animals they made their way back to the camp. They were quiet in case others wanted to hang out by the water. In no time, however, the other tribes all followed them back.

Just before dark they heard a commotion over toward the meadow and quickly moved together to see what they might discover. A whole flock of turkeys were milling around, communicating in the way that turkeys do.

It seemed they must have been talking about the elk who was eating from the lower branches on the far corner of the meadow, and perhaps whether he was worth fearing. Apparently, they decided he wasn't, for they continued foraging through the tall grasses. In their excitement about the elk, they never heard the tribes coming, not exactly noiselessly, from the campsite.

Zach was happy to still be holding his camera.

After returning to the camp, they sat in a circle around the fire and discussed the wildlife they had seen. Pete reiterated that which he had spoken to his group. The other tribes had to admit that they had forgotten to consider the deer as perspective enemies, but had no trouble viewing the wolves as such. Oops! The truth is, you see, is that most of them had forgotten they were watchmen as soon as the animals had come into sight.

Suddenly it occurred to Mr. Jack that they seemed to have totally lost track of what day of the week it was. A Sunday had come and gone and no one had taken notice of it.

"Fellow heathens," said Mr. Jack forcefully, but with a smile. "It seems that we have forgotten to acknowledge that it was Sunday, and held no formal church service. Do you think the LORD will forgive us?"

Surprise registered on each face. "Imagine that," said Randy. "I never gave it a thought. It seems as though this time together has been one extended church service and celebration of life."

"My point is this," continued Mr. Jack. "Would to God that life was like this all the time. We would be totally caught up with the mindset and purposes of God so much that every day would be like a Sunday. Of course, that is not possible in most people's world, but out here it has been different for our group. I'm sure that the LORD has not held it against us. I feel no conviction or guilt at all, as we have been sharing constant and close communion with Him.

Randy is right and, for the record, I wouldn't exchange what we've had here for anything. I am not trying in any way to take away from the need to attend church services; in fact, the Bible says it is a must. We need the fellowship, to hear the Word, and to saturate ourselves in the purposes of God. And that day of rest is necessary for adults and children, and is a gift from God.

But now, let us pray together, break a little bread, and imagine our water to be the juice of the fruit of the vine, before we turn in. I believe the LORD will honor our celebration of His sacrifice. What do you say?"

Everyone 'Amened' his suggestion with fervor. Randy went to the wagon to get some sourdough bread that they might break together.

The fire in the center of the circle seemed to add to their service, something deeper than words can express.

Mr. Jack shared the text from First Corinthians, chapter eleven, even as Paul had spoken it to the church.

They prayed, broke bread, and drank the juice of the rock itself: crystal clear water. The weary watchmen headed for their tents, contented and well-filled.

Chapter Twenty-seven

The Manner of Manna

The four woke to the sound of the shofar the following morning. They had talked of getting up early and sneaking down to the river to see if they might spot some wild animals, but, that wasn't going to happen.

As Josiah went to greet Mustgofast and bring him for water, he noticed that this spot was alive with activity. Birds and insects alike sounded as though they were trying to outdo each other. It sounded like a wildlife or bird sanctuary.

He felt great this morning after a delicious night's rest. "How are you, Mustgo?" he asked, affectionately using the horse's nickname and ruffling his mane. Mustgofast, of course, acknowledged his question with a nudge and a smile.

They headed for the water where Josiah made ready for the day. He lay on his stomach on the shore and then splashed water on his face. It felt cool and refreshing.

As he picked up his head to rise to his feet, he saw across the water on the edge of the woods, from the same spot as yesterday, the doe with her fawn.

He did not move a muscle. Of course there was no way to warn Mustgofast, who was busily cropping the tender shoots of grass further behind Josiah, up on the bank, having already had his fill of water.

Even as yesterday the doe walked the path alone at first, slowly out a ways before turning back to encourage her fawn to proceed to the water's edge. It appeared she hadn't noticed either of them there.

Back at camp everyone was getting up with the normal sounds of activity, not considering that the doe might be here. For that matter, of course, neither had he. The noise didn't stop the deer, however. She proceeded, though cautiously, with her young charge that bolted down the path, apparently without a care in the world.

Josiah lay as though paralyzed while directly across from him the little one drank as the attentive mother kept her watch. When the fawn had finished, the mother drank quickly. It appeared to him that she stuck her whole face into the water so she could guzzle what she needed in a hurry.

The little one was beautiful. How Josiah would have loved to have him, or her, for a pet at home. The doe looked so gentle and like such a caring mother. He was thankful that God had heard his prayer and spared these two. He knew they wouldn't live forever, but he was glad that their days were not up.

Even as he had with the eagle, he wondered how it must feel to be a deer. It seemed they always looked nervous; never quite relaxed. Though they were beautiful, he couldn't imagine that there was much fun for them. He decided that not for a moment would he want to be a deer - an eagle, for five minutes maybe, yes - but a deer, not for a minute, though for sure they were very graceful animals. He decided that in the long run, even as with humans, beauty counted for little.

"Hey, Siah!" shouted Zachary as he headed toward the water with his camera. "We probably won't see any animals, but I brought my camera, just in case. It's late now though. All the animals, I'm sure, have already been down to the water to drink. Tomorrow we'll have to get up earlier and sneak down."

Or course, the deer were long gone at the warning sound of his approach. Though Siah was a little disappointed that no one else had seen them, he was thankful and felt privileged that he had.

"You just missed yesterday's doe and her fawn right across from me. She came from the same spot as yesterday. I watched them drink. They ran when they heard you coming."

"Oops," said Zach apologetically, "sorry, Siah."

"No, that's OK," he answered. "They were just leaving anyway. They couldn't stay long."

By now many of the others were down by the water, including Pete, and Josiah shared how he had watched the deer and how God had spared them the fate of being food at the wolves' banquet.

"She probably waited intentionally this morning," said Randy, "until she felt the wolves and the more aggressive wildlife had drunk their fill. She's no dummy. Earlier, right at dawn, I imagine, there would have been greater danger for her and her little one." Josiah was glad that the mother had been so wise.

They stayed in that place for three days and nights; investigating all that they felt was worthwhile. On the last night, Mr. Jack spoke to the tribes about what came next for the Israelites.

"After they left Elim they came to the Wilderness of Sin," he began. "They had left Rameses in Egypt exactly one month earlier and had now run out of food. Of course you must know who they blamed for their lack of provisions."

One of the boys from the tribe of Asher called out, "Moses and Aaron!"

"You're right," Mr. Jack continued. "As they became hungry they started again to wish they had stayed back in Egypt, much like many of us do as soon as the going gets tough; as though it were easy in Egypt.

They saw the wilderness as one big cemetery with absolutely no hope of opportunity, rather than all that the LORD had done.

And so, the LORD rained bread down from heaven. They called it *manna*, which means, *'what is it?'* The LORD further said that He would put them to the test as to whether they would obey His ways or not. He spoke through Moses and Aaron very simply, just how they were to gather their heavenly provision.

Even as Aaron spoke the people looked toward the wilderness and saw a cloud which was the presence of the LORD. But, you see, even at that the people complained and wanted meat. I'm sure most of you have heard the story.

God had spoken to them to gather the manna in the morning, each day, and to leave none overnight or for the sun to beat upon, but for the day before the Sabbath God would give them two days' portion.

They were lazy, or whatever, and left some of it, even overnight, and the next day there were worms on it. It is not for us to leave today's portion overnight or

Satan, that is Beelzebub, the lord of the flies, will see to it that it quickly becomes infested with his babies. Believe me when I tell you they are not cute. The common housefly for example, hatches in twenty-four hours. He does not need much time to populate.

When they wanted meat, God caused a great wind to come in and blew in quail as far as the eye could see; surrounding the camp of the Israelites. Even as they greedily gathered it and stuffed it into their mouths the anger of the LORD had been kindled and before they even swallowed it, many choked to death. No Heimlich maneuver or CPR could have saved them.

It is a very sad, but typical, report of the condition and nature of man, when we never quite have enough.

The LORD, of course, does the same with us. The New Testament Manna is Jesus Christ. He is the Bread of Heaven. Many complain without even realizing it, that He is not sufficient and that what they have is not enough.

We must be careful or we, like the Israelites, come into the same fate and may well choke on those things that we thought were necessary or life could simply not go on. So often we take our eyes off the Manna and put them on those things outside of our reach in a lustful way."

As he paused, many, especially the adults who had lived a bit more of life and recognized in themselves the truth of Mr. Jack's words, quietly agreed, "Amen".

Chapter Twenty-eight

Come Thirsty

The next day the group left the beautiful Elim. Though they had enjoyed it very much, everyone was eager to see what lie ahead.

It was warmer and without the cool breezes as they traveled away from the water and into an area that was not quite so lush and green.

As the day progressed they were soon surrounded again by the browns and greys that testified of little water. They saw only a few ground animals and vultures. Again they had been warned to go easy on the drinking water, for they could not be sure where and when they would next come across a brook or stream. For as far as the eye could see there was nothing now but the bleak starkness of the lack of green.

Josiah said, matter-of-factly, "After this trip, I think that green is going to be my favorite color. Until this time it was blue." Everyone who heard him chuckled at the profoundness of his reasoning.

"Keep in mind, boys," Mr. Jack shared when they stopped for a piece of jerky, "that it was the LORD Who was leading the Israelites. The people were still being guided by the cloud by day and the fire by night. They did not go anywhere until they were directed to move.

I must say it was probably more from fear of being alone in this strange place than from trust and honor. How that must break the heart of God when after He has proven Himself so many times, we still fail to trust. No doubt, they would have been terrified to lag behind or go ahead of that which represented the presence of God.

Most of them probably had no holy excitement or anticipation of what might come tomorrow or what the future might hold. They were so locked into the past. Perhaps the youth held onto some hope, as youth sometimes has a way of doing even when everything seems bleak. But, under the constant attack of discouragement and pessimism it is more likely that it was probably *only* the grace of God because of His promise to Abraham, Isaac, and Jacob that even kept the youth. But for that, more than likely, few would have made it to the Promised Land of Canaan.

Today, there are many who fail to grab ahold of the promises of God for the same reason. They forget what the LORD has done, moving from one crisis to another. They take for granted the cloud by day and the fire by night, and fail to see how miraculous the presence of the LORD really is. It is easier to lose sight of these things today than it was back then, because today there are so many more distractions."

In spite of the discipline of rationing their water it was not long before their supply ran dry. "I don't know if it's because I know we're out of water," Juanito said to Josiah, "but I can't ever remember being this thirsty."

"I know what you mean," Siah said. "Man, I can hardly swallow."

"Look!" one of the older boys shouted, "There's a sign!"

It was strange that in his thirst, Josiah had forgotten to keep his eyes open for the next marker for a stopping place. Apparently, everyone else had forgotten too. Even stranger, is that no one ran to be the first one there.

It was late afternoon. Mustgofast seemed like he might be a little thirsty too. Josiah wondered, but dared not to ask him so as not to remind him of what he might have managed to take his mind off. He had decided that it was best if he didn't even mention it.

As they came closer to the sign, they noticed that behind it looked to be a hill. All that could be seen was a rock ledge, huge and jagged, and nothing but the far-off mountains, green and inviting, way off in the distance.

"You want to go read the sign?" Pete asked Josiah.

Quickly Josiah with Mustgofast hurried to the sign, almost forgetting his thirst, eager to see what might be over the top of this rise which covered the whole of the immediate horizon. While they were walking he had noticed it, but thought it to be a mirage, as the light and heat against the ground had fooled him many times.

"It says, **Rephidim,**" he said, loud enough that everyone might hear.

He reached in the plastic pocket in the back and handed out the journeymen's cards. As he gave them out Mustgofast remained by the sign talking softly to his boy about what was over the hill. The little mustang kept his eyes toward the crest of the hill and continued to make throaty sounds even as Siah handed out the cards.

Pete had to smile at the communication between the horse and Josiah. It was remarkable, he thought.

Mustgofast made absolutely no attempt to walk to the top of the hill, though, for sure, he might have and no one would have faulted him for it. He waited, though a bit impatiently it seemed, for his boy.

"In this place," began Mr. Jack, as Josiah continued, "the people again became angry with Moses, for they had no water. The name *Rephidim* literally means: *railed in* and a specific *place of refreshing.*

You see, the people, including the children, and the animals were thirsty. To all appearances it looked like there was no water for as far as the eye could see.

Even if there were some over in those mountains, it looks too far away to even make the distance between us. Again, they failed to see that all things were possible with God. It doesn't matter how things appear, how they feel, or how they seem.

And, again the Israelites asked Moses if he had taken them out into the wilderness to die; to kill them and their children. Can you imagine the frustration of this man? There was no doubt that if God hadn't helped him he was not up to the challenge of these people, even as many pastors, missionaries, and leaders today. Good leadership is pricey; the leader must invest much of himself in order to be long-suffering as the LORD requires. It may look like fun as we look on to the one who holds the microphone or the final decision, but *godly* leadership is purchased with much sacrifice and humility or it is not *godly* at all.

How glorious the story plays out. It is one of my favorites, as even in my own life I have witnessed parallels. The LORD told Moses to take his staff and to go to the rock. He said that He would be standing upon the Rock, right in front of Moses. This Rock was part of Mt. Horeb, which is part of Mt. Sinai, where Moses would later receive the Ten Commandments. The name *Horeb* translates: *a dry an arid place by reason of a drought.* How significant is that? Now, I've been in many places like that. But any time I have truly turned my face to the Rock, that is, Jesus, for help, He has never let me down, and water has poured onto me from under the door of His throne. And that's the truth! He has never failed."

Mr. Jack stopped as though reflecting for a time, on instances of refreshing and healing. It was a wonderful silence even as all the other adults visited times when they had been at Mt. Horeb and the LORD had seen them through. Some of the children visited that place in their minds too, though most of them simply basked in the reflection of it from the face of the adults.

"And so Moses smote the Rock and water poured forth; right out of the Rock. And Moses named the place Massah, for temptation, and Meribah, for striving.

It was here where the Israelites fought their first battle against the Amalekites. Moses told Joshua that he would stand with his staff upon the hill. And, it was here that Aaron and Hur held up the arms of Moses, for when the rod was lifted up, Israel prevailed, and when it was dropped, the Amalekites prevailed. Moses realized that he needed help to win the battle. He could not do it alone. Even in the book of Genesis, God spoke that it was not good that man should be alone. It is not His plan."

With this Randy began to connect-the-dots again in his own life. He had isolated himself in the past five years since Sylvie had died. The words of Jack Harris bore witness deep in his spirit. "No one man is the answer," he thought. "God has created us to need each other; both to give and to take. Each of us is meant to be part of the bigger picture."

And, as he reflected he wondered how many times someone may have needed him, and he wasn't there. He had had no right to withhold that which he had already, those years ago, given to the LORD when first he said, "Use me, LORD." My goodness, what had he been thinking?

"After the battle was won," continued Mr. Jack, "the LORD spoke to Moses to write the account of it in a book to be remembered and read to Joshua, and that the LORD would remove Amalek from off the face of the earth. Amalek, you see, is a descendant of Esau. Remember the Word tells us that God hated Esau. These are those who take no pleasure in the LORD, or the people of God, and those things that He has done for those who love Him. One day the God-haters will no longer even be remembered under heaven."

Now, all the time that Mr. Jack spoke, which wasn't long, it seemed everyone had forgotten his thirst. Certainly it wasn't possible that Mustgofast had forgotten too, but, there he stood, respectfully waiting for his master Josiah without a sound.

"It was at this point," continued Mr. Jack, "after the battle was won, that Moses built an altar. He called it **Jehovahnissi**, which, interpreted means, *The LORD my banner.*

Now," he said, "come around this side of the rock between it and the top of the hill."

There stood a banner, high, and waving as it furled in the breezes coming from the other side of the hill. It said, **Jehovahnissi - *The LORD my banner*.** There was something about it that made Josiah feel like crying and he struggled not to give in to it.

Everyone stood quiet at the sight of it for a short time. Finally, the silence was broken by the clear long blast of the shofar. Juanito blew it several times.

"The descendants of Esau, those who count the work of the Cross as nothing, don't stand a chance," said Randy "as long as we come thirsty."

Chapter Twenty-nine

Remember Me?

Mr. Jack lifted his staff and hit the rock, looking up as though he might truly be able to see the LORD. "Now, look," he said, "over the crest of this hill. Imagine that what you see there came from this Rock and flowed onto a dry and thirsty land. I have not seen the view from the top myself, but with the job that Pete and Joshua did, I know that it will bear witness to this text."

Everyone hurried to the top; children and adults alike. From the ridge they could see down the hill and into the greenest of valleys. Meandering along the bottom was a beautiful winding stream. It was as though the LORD had taken His finger and run it through soft putty or child's clay from the mountain and down through the base of the valley, like a squiggle under a signature, just to add some finishing touch. It was amazing how that one side of the hill was brown and appeared so lifeless, while just over the crest was a lush green and fertile land.

"Can we go down there, Mr. Jack?" asked one of the boys after a moment of silence.

"What are we waiting for?" returned Mr. Jack. "We'll camp down there by the water."

Down they all rushed; Josiah and Mustgofast in the lead. Though some of the older boys could have passed them, out of respect no one attempted to steal what seemed to be his spot, at least in this place.

Again, the water from this stream ran from the mountain looming a little northeast from where they were. The rippling waters glistened in the sunlight and seemed to sing out an invitation to come and partake. Mustgofast was the first to plunge his face into the water. Three feet upstream, Josiah lay on his stomach with his face in the water.

"The water has a sweet taste," said Juanito. "Do you notice it, Josiah?" he asked through the translator.

"Yes, I do," Josiah answered. "It really does."

Randy, who had overheard the boys from close by could have said many things, but, at the risk of sounding hyper spiritual, he kept them to himself.

Inside however, he was having a private audience with the LORD, for he too had noticed the sweetness of the water as he drank deeply from his cupped hands. He thought that perhaps it was the greatest water he had ever tasted.

"It was in this place that Moses was reunited with his wife, his two sons, and his father-in-law by the mountain of God," Mr. Jack explained as he sat on the bank of the stream after drinking his fill. "And, it was at this time that Jethro, Moses' father-in-law, spoke to Moses about his need for assistance, and about the fact that he was undertaking to do too much on his own. Like the rest of us, Moses needed help.

And over there," here Mr. Jack pointed toward the mountain not far off in the distance, "is Mt. Sinai, where Moses later received the Ten Commandments and the law from the LORD.

It is here that the 'rubber meets the road', so to speak, between Judaism and Christianity, because Jesus is the fulfillment of all that was given to Moses in this place. They called it the Mountain of God. That's pretty tremendous, huh?" Now the reader must certainly know that everyone agreed.

"Fire came down from the LORD as He descended upon this mountain, and then the smoke ascended toward the heavens. The earth quaked and the people trembled with fear. The Bible says the sound of the trumpet sounded long and louder and louder from the heavens and then the LORD spoke to Moses. That is the God we serve today in the person of Jesus Christ; the One Who lives inside those who serve Him.

And it was there," Mr. Jack continued, pointing with his staff as though this were actually Mt. Sinai, "that God gave Moses instructions regarding the building of the tabernacle and the Ark of the Covenant that would house the presence of God.

The LORD spoke tenderly as He told Moses that He would be the God of Israel and dwell among them.

And while Moses was on the mountain hearing from the King of Creation, the people right down here (Mr. Jack swung his staff around to include the whole valley below) built, under the direction of Aaron, a golden calf to worship. It is a heartbreaking account for sure."

"Is that why the people had to wander the wilderness for forty years, Mr. Jack?" asked one of the boys.

"No," he answered. "They were only in their third month out of Egypt; actually I believe it was fifty days after Passover. It was the original Pentecost.

Shortly after that time just a short distance from this place, they sent spies into the Promised Land, Canaan. These came back with a report of fertile lands and fruitful crops, but of giants and men many times their superiors and of their fear of them.

They had forgotten about God and His provision again. This time, however, God would not tolerate it and told them that the older generation would not enter in, but that they would all die in the wilderness.

The people as a whole would spend one year wandering for every day they had spent spying out the land of Canaan. They were there for forty days, and so, except for Joshua and Caleb, forty years later only the younger generation would cross the Jordan River and enter in. What a horrible price to pay for their unbelief and their lack of trust in their Creator. God had given them so much, and would hold them accountable for it. So many times they had witnessed miracles and received directly from the hand of God. They may have even noticed it and given God the glory for it at the time, but the problem was that, like us, they failed to remember.

They had partaken of God's protection from the plagues in Egypt. They had seen the parting of the Red Sea and witnessed its closing, as it swallowed up those enemies of God. They had benefited from the guidance and shelter of a cloud by day and a fire by night.

When they were thirsty, water had poured forth from a rock. When they ran out of food, bread rained down from heaven. God had sweetened the water when it was too bitter to swallow. More than anything else, however, He had been long-suffering and gracious through all their complaining and fault-finding."

It grew quiet as everyone digested the words of Mr. Jack; most of them looking into the water or to the mountain, each lost in his own thoughts.

"Well, my friend," Randy spoke to Mr. Jack, finally breaking the silence. "You just gave my testimony again, loud and clear. God has always been there for me even when I failed to see it, or to give Him glory for His provision. What must I have been thinking?

Don't answer that. I know what I was thinking. 'Poor me ~ does anyone have to bear what I am carrying? I know You are there, LORD, even though I can't see You.' Now, as you are talking, Brother Jack, it is amazing that I never saw Him, because He really was there, holding me up; living and breathing; right there, in the midst of my difficult times. It could have been so different if I had taken the time to notice and to remember.

It is obvious to me now that self-pity is pretty much a destroyer. It wants little to do with truth, avoids the mirror at all costs, and travels only with companions much like itself. Man, what a bummer!"

"If it's any consolation, Randy," Mr. Jack responded, "That's probably the testimony of at least every adult within hearing distance, sometime or another."

A quiet "Amen" of conviction from the adults confirmed that what Mr. Jack had said was true.

Chapter Thirty

A View from the Top

"Hello!" someone called from over the hill.

"Hey, it's Joshua!" shouted Pete. "Hey, Josh!" he greeted as he scrambled to his feet and hurried toward his brother.

"Well, I'll be," smiled Patty, "look who's here, Jack."

Over the hill came Joshua on a horse and smiling from ear-to-ear. "I made it after all," he said. "My plans changed so I hoped you wouldn't mind if I joined you all for the rest of the trip. I don't know, but I really felt prompted to come spend some time with you guys and not to miss out on at least a part of the tour. Is that OK?"

"I'm real glad you're here, Josh. Hey, everyone," said Mr. Jack, as he walked forward to greet him, "meet my other son, Joshua." Then he spoke to Josh, "Everyone's been told how you helped Pete map out this trip and the stopping places. You guys did a tremendous job. We've been having a great time. Sure glad you could join us." Mrs. Patty too, of course, had walked over and was obviously very happy that he was here.

"Before I forget," said Josh, getting down now from his horse, "who's Josiah?"

Shyly Siah lifted his hand in acknowledgment of Josh's question. "Come on over here," said Mr. Jack, motioning with his hand to encourage Josiah.

"Well, I'm pleased to meet you. I've heard so much about you. Someone asked me to give you something," Josh continued. "It's from Randy and was supposed to be in the chuck wagon with the other stuff. It's your lasso from last year. Apparently, he saved it for you and wanted you to have it."

Josiah's shyness left him as his excitement about the lasso took over. "Wow, thanks!" he said enthusiastically. "Hey, Juanito," he said, looking back at his now close friend. "How do you say *lasso* in Spanish?"

"Reata," answered Juanito, not needing an interpreter to understand the question. The three didn't wait to walk away from the crowd that Josiah might practice throwing the rope around a rock (the three, of course, being Siah, Juanito, and Mustgofast). He was awkward at first, but much of what he had learned last year quickly came back to him.

Of course Juanito had his shots at it, but no one else even asked, not wanting to take any fun away from Josiah.

Mustgofast stood still for a time while Josiah attempted to lasso his neck with the rope. It didn't appear that he was enjoying it, but for the sake of his boy he had obviously made the decision to be longsuffering.

The plan was that after lunch the group would spend time exploring again, as the leaders saw fit.

As they were setting up camp though, Randy told Mr. Jack that he would like to go back over the crest of the hill again, and climb up on the high jagged rock above where the sign was, just to discover how far he could see from its peak. The formation looked to be about fifty feet high. "I should be back in less than an hour," he said, "and it doesn't appear steep at all. It looks to ascend very gradually on the north side. Would you think me irresponsible?" he asked Mr. Jack. "I'm not abandoning the team or the cooking."

"No," Mr. Jack responded quickly, "That'll be fine. We are three other leaders for the Levites and now Josh is here besides. Go ahead, but be careful to take your whistle along just in case you want to call us."

"No problem, but, don't forget, I was born and grew up in this country. Guess there really isn't much that would take me by surprise. And," he continued, "I'm used to being alone." Randy was not proud of that but, nevertheless, he knew it to be true. "This time though, I won't be feeling sorry for myself," he smiled.

"Can we go with you?" asked Josiah hurriedly. "I think Mustgofast could climb the back of that rock. I noticed it before. It goes up very gradually." Mr. Jack almost spoke up, but for some reason he held back.

Immediately Juanito added his voice to Josiah's. "Me too?" he asked in broken English.

No one else from the Levites came forward because no one else wanted to climb. They were happy to have 'landed' where they were and contented to sit around the water for a while, basking in the beauty of this place and enjoying each other's company.

"OK," answered Randy. "No problem; you can come."

The truth was though that Randy had really wanted to go alone, but didn't have the heart to refuse the boys. After all, he had volunteered to chaperone the boys; this trip was really all about them-wasn't it?

So, off they went back up over the crest of the hill. Mustgofast was raring to go; Josiah had his lasso in hand, Randy his staff; and Juanito walked briskly as though they had been resting all day. Each of them, including the horse, it seemed, was eager to explore the rock.

They weren't concerned this time about any need to whisper, for they felt there would be no animals to scare off in this arid, brown, desert of a place.

Up over the crest they went, eager to see what view might unfold from the peak of this rock formation;

the boys comfortable in the company of their friend Randy. Neither Josiah nor Juanito gave it a thought that the interpreter was not with them. They were determined that somehow they would make it work. They were pleasantly surprised when they discovered that many things could be expressed without words, and, what's more, they were having fun trying to communicate. It had become like a game and neither was frustrated in their attempts. At first they had felt awkward and rather shy to even try, but that had quickly disappeared as their friendship grew.

Even as they suspected, the climb presented no challenge for the little mustang. Josiah had his lasso wound now and draped over one shoulder, while he held Mustgofast's lead rope. This he did more for encouragement than for any other reason. He wasn't exactly sure if it was security more for him or for Mustgo, but, in any event, it felt good to hold the rope.

The rock seemed to grow a little steeper toward the top; nevertheless, Mustgofast persisted with little effort it seemed to make it all the way.

Immediately they were glad they had come for the view was stupendous. Off in the distance they could see the campers and their tents, like so many animated toy figures. Smoke was already curling skyward from the two fires which had been started.

To the north loomed the range of mountains; the Rockies, of course. They stood like sentinels over the valley; defying anyone to disturb the scene playing out below.

"I wish I'd thought to ask Zachary to let me borrow his camera," said Randy. "This spot is simply breathtaking. Look around, boys."

It made Josiah a little nervous to see how closely Randy had walked now toward the peak that jutted out over the rocky ground below. He didn't feel it was necessary that he himself or Mustgofast should come any closer to the peak than where they were to have a great view. He could see that Juanito felt the same way as they hung back about fifteen feet from the edge. Josiah was thankful that the little mustang did not make any attempt to move closer, but hung right by his side, and thankful also that Randy made no attempt to coerce the boys out further.

Now, the whole area atop the rock was flat, much like a small plateau. It was large enough that Josiah felt a helicopter could land comfortably on it if necessary. Both boys slowly turned three hundred, sixty degrees to take in the entirety of the view. There was no doubt that it was gorgeous.

"Maybe we can come back up before we leave," suggested Josiah to Randy, "with Zach's camera and take some pictures. Maybe he'll even want to come with us. He would like this view a lot."

Josiah thought how Randy looked strangely like a painting of Moses that he had seen. In the painting Moses was standing with his staff in his outstretched hand as God parted the Red Sea. Actually, Josiah had thought before how much the character of Randy reminded him of what Joshua, the man who followed Moses so faithfully and later, after Moses died, lead the people across the Jordan River and into the Promised Land. Josiah liked the character of Joshua in the Bible.

As Randy turned to respond to Josiah's suggestion about returning later, out of a crevice not two feet from where he was standing reared up a huge rattlesnake. Startled, Randy stepped back without thinking, throwing his staff toward the snake. Equally startled, the snake slithered down the rock, but, not before Randy lost his balance and fell off the edge of the high, jagged precipice.

Both boys screamed as they bolted into action. Randy had managed to grab ahold of the sharp overhanging rocks and dangled fifty feet above the ground below.

"Help me!" he screamed in agony as blood from the sharp cuts he had received in both palms already ran down his arms. "I can't hold onto the rock!"

Quickly Juanito sprang into action and grabbing up the staff he laid it so that about one foot of its over five foot length hung out over the edge between Randy's two hands. Then, he went close to the other end of the staff and stood upon it.

Immediately, Josiah could see what his plan was. "Randy!" Josiah shouted, unafraid now to come close to the edge that his friend might hear him. "See if you can grab the staff. It's right between your hands!"

Juanito could not see what was going on and dared not move a muscle, and Josiah was petrified as he lay on his stomach trying to assist his friend to let go of the sharp edge and grab the overhanging rod.

"Don't move, Juanito," he cautioned. Though his Mexican friend did not understand the English words spoken by Josiah, there it was again: that language that is clearer than the spoken word that comes from within. He understood clearly.

"Help me, Jesus," prayed Josiah as he reached out for the wrist of his friend Randy; Josiah now dangling over the edge far more than he was comfortable with. The sharpness of the rock was against his chest right at his armpits. He didn't care if he cut himself doing it; he intended to save Randy.

Grabbing Randy's right wrist now, Josiah held with all his might and both hands to assist him to grab the staff. It was by the grace of God and that only, that Randy was able to let go with one hand and make a clumsy but successful grab for the staff. Quickly and without Josiah's help, he was then able to grab with the other hand.

"Josiah," he said, "I don't have the strength to pull myself up."

"Just hold on," Josiah answered him with more confidence than he felt. "Everything will be OK. Don't let go," he said, petrified not only by the circumstances, but by the steady flow of blood trailing down Randy's arms.

Quickly Josiah stood and unfurled the lasso still wrapped around his shoulder. He lay again upon the rock and reached over the edge. With force he swirled the end with the loop on it two or three times, trying to encircle Randy's upper body, under his arms and then grab the loop. Finally, he managed to catch the end of it and work the rope through the loop.

He stood now with the free end gripped tightly in his hands. "Come here, Mustgo," he said. "Hurry, but be careful." The horse, as though he understood every word, walked forward. When he came within four feet of the edge, Josiah continued. "OK, boy, stop."

Siah wrapped the rope securely around Mustgofast's neck and then walked back to the edge to talk with Randy.

"I can't hold on anymore," whispered Randy. "Thanks for everything, especially for this trip. I'm so sorry you have to see this."

"It's OK," said Josiah. "You're tied to Mustgofast and you're not going to fall. Get ready to climb."

"OK, Mustgo," he commanded to the waiting mustang. "Back up slowly."

Mustgofast understood that command which was very common to him, even at the ranch; never mind in this circumstance. With little effort, it seemed, he obeyed his master and began to step backwards. If this didn't work, it wouldn't be because he hadn't done what Josiah had told him to do.

In seconds Randy lay atop the rock crying and thanking God that he hadn't come up here alone. And, as he wept, all he could say was, "Thank You, Father."

Chapter Thirty-one

Grace, Grace!

After a time, the boys helped Randy onto the back of Mustgofast and together they headed back to the camp.

As they crested the ridge of the hill, heading back, many spotted them coming and, of course, wondered at Randy sitting on top of Mustgofast with Josiah leading. Juanito walked along with Randy's staff by their side.

Though everyone was curious now, no one was overly concerned, for it was obvious that Randy looked fine. Indeed, most thought they must be playing some joke since Randy wore a smile; the two escorting him on the horse as though they were his subjects, and he some prince or king.

The distance and the ride between the rock and the camp had settled Randy's nerves and he was, but for the cuts on his hands, none the worse for wear. The group spoke little on their way to join the others, as all of them had been traumatized. As soon as they got closer to the camp, however, everyone noticed that what they thought to be dirt from the rock was in fact blood on Randy's arms and clothes.

When they arrived into the camp Josiah simply announced, "He's OK." He let go of Mustgofast's lead rope and ran now toward Mr. Jack. He threw his arms around him and burst out crying. Mr. Jack asked no questions, knowing that he needed a moment and that all would be talked over later. He simply cried with him, his own tears spilling out atop Josiah's sun-bleached hair.

Pete and Joshua were helping Randy off the horse while Mrs. Patty moved quickly to Juanito, also crying now, as he held tightly to the blood-soaked staff. The rest of the group stared; unable to imagine what must have taken place.

Randy insisted on being led down to the river that he might take off his shoes and socks and wade into the crystal mountain stream. He would change his clothes after, and they would all sit and listen to his story.

When they had gathered their wits about them, Juan and Josiah changed into shorts and jumped into the water to be free from the dirt, grime, and blood of the trial they had just come through.

"Come on, Mustgo!" remembered Josiah. "Hey, you're a hero, too, you know. Come on in with us!"

The little mustang needed no more coercion as he headed down to the water to join his boy. The two boys splashed water over the horse's back to cool him. He liked it, even as he whispered to Josiah, and played with them until they left the water.

In fifteen minutes the three were all sitting on the bank enjoying being served their lunch by those who recognized that they had been through a difficult time. Everyone was eager to hear and not a one was absent from the circle that surrounded them. Everything else could wait.

Randy began their story after he first asked the boys if they wished to share it with the group. Both of them were more than happy to decline and simply to eat their beans, which, by the way, never tasted so good, and to hear the telling of it.

For sure, Mustgofast wasn't talking. He was cropping the tender grass which grew along the bank and all the way back into the tent area. He seemed totally disinterested in what the group might be saying or listening to, even if they talked about him. He simply kept about what he considered to be his business with an attitude that clearly reflected his opinion, 'you had to be there'.

As he told the story, Randy could not help but being overwhelmed by the parallels to the battles and the walk in the lives of Christians. As he put it into words, on several occasions, he was overcome by his emotions and had to stop for a bit in order to continue on.

First of all, there was the coming of Joshua with the lasso. That, he knew, was only the grace of God. Then there was his attempt to go alone and the request of

Josiah and Juanito to go with him. Again, that was God's grace. Even the fact that his friend Jack hadn't tried to stop them at that time seemed very curious to him. That was another measure of grace.

"God was looking after me right to the finest details," he continued. "Right from the start the fact that the men made me a staff too, was only the grace of God. Who could ever charge any one of these things, much less, so many, to coincidence? It is mind-blowing, I tell you!"

Mr. Jack chuckled to himself at the preacher who had been unleashed in the passion of Random Mann. He felt privileged and humbled to witness it, to be a part of it, and to see how God could use the plan of a child again.

"And the fact that Josiah even took Mustgofast to the top of that rock is uncanny," Randy continued. "And to think about how unsuspecting I was is a whole message in itself, Brother Jack. Man, that'll preach!

In my arrogance I let you know how familiar I was with the territory, as though that made me exempt from attack. That old serpent quickly took advantage of that as I dropped my guard and stood dangerously close to the edge of the precipice. Is there a clearer message than that? What a lack of wisdom I showed and how I've been busted!" at this Randy smiled. "It is all nothing but the grace of God I tell you, and, as far as I'm concerned; the icing on the cake."

He turned then to Josiah and Juanito. "I only hope I haven't marred you boys for life. That must have been a horrible thing to see. I thank you so much for being so responsible, for moving so quickly, and for saving my life. I shall never forget it."

The translator talked softly to Juanito even as he himself was all choked up and barely able to mouth the words.

"It was the LORD Who helped us," said Josiah, "all of us! I'm glad He was there with us. I was scared out of my wits."

Through the translator, Juanito shared about how frightened he was that his feet would slip and Randy would plunge to his death. There was no doubt in their minds that without a miracle Randy never would have made it off the edge and back up onto the solid rock.

"Thank God for friends!" Randy said. "But for His grace I would not have been saved."

Chapter Thirty-two

The Promised Land

The following morning, though they were surprised, the boys were awakened early by the sound of the shofar as Juanito blew it.

Quickly, at just about six, everyone scrambled to attention and assembled with their tribes; all still in their night clothes. The last they had heard the night before was that they would be able to sleep in today.

Immediately Josiah wondered if Randy's hands had gotten worse. There was Randy though, outside his own tent, and looking relaxed from his night's sleep. He waved over at the boys as he surmised what might be going through their minds, and they stood at ease.

"We will be pulling out this morning," announced Mr. Jack. "I know it's early, but there has been a change of plans. Today, we will cross over the Jordan River and enter into the Promised Land. We are not cutting your time short, but only this leg of it, so, let's get ready to move. Breakfast is waiting. You will have bread, jerky, and water. For the adults; coffee is on. Now let's go!"

Everyone was charged by the order that could not be interpreted another way and the seeming need for haste. They would be on the move, no doubt, in half-an-hour.

Randy was fine this morning, though his bandaged hands were sore of course. Josiah's arms were aching, but he felt not to mention it except to the three boys, Juanito, and, of course, Mustgofast. Juanito's upper leg muscles were sore. He made the same face that Josiah had made regarding his upper arm and chest muscles, so they understood each other clearly as Josiah interpreted for Juanito to the group, as though that needed interpretation. The pain was probably due more to stress than the physical strain, as both of them had been so tense during the whole ordeal. Neither could even imagine how Randy's muscles must ache.

They continued to walk northeast throughout the morning through the green meadows and sparse wooded areas. At around eleven down the hill and just across the meadow they spotted what must be their Jordan River. It was the first time they had seen manmade buildings since they had come into the wilderness. Most of them had mixed feelings about it.

"Of course," Mr. Jack said, as they sat down for some water and jerky, "I am sure we don't feel quite like the Israelites would have when at last their forty year trek was finished. We cannot even relate. Most of you, I would guess, may even be a little disappointed to see signs of civilization across the Jordan.

That beautiful ranch up there is the home of Random Mann, and it is the place where we will finish up our time here.

He has offered to allow us a bit of a reprieve from our journey and last night phoned some of his friends in the church to make ready for our return. For the next four days we will enjoy the land of milk and honey. Is that OK?"

Just as quickly as it had shown up, their disappointment left, unable to live in this place of optimism and hope. The green meadows across the water were speckled with sheep, cattle, and horses. Already Mustgofast had his ears perked up at the sight, or maybe the smell of the place.

"Can Mustgofast stay?" asked Josiah, suddenly concerned for his buddy. He didn't want to have to part company with him before it was necessary.

"You bet he can," answered Randy quickly. "He'll get the best grain that money can buy. He can stay until you have to leave, Siah."

No one spent much time in crossing the Jordan, even though Mr. Jack tried to gain their attention in the story of that great parting of the water at the hands of Joshua.

"It is clear," Mr. Jack had said, "that at this point Moses' ministry is done. I can barely keep your attention; much less get you to focus on anything I'm saying. Your eyes are all over on the Promised Land. See that hill over there?" he asked. "That's Mt. Nebo, where God gave Moses a view of the Promised Land before he died at the age of one hundred, twenty years old and then buried him. I guess my role as Moses is over.

And so," he said, smiling, "Joshua, that is, Randy, will have to take it from here if that's OK with him."

Now the reader must certainly remember Josiah's thoughts of how Randy reminded him of that man Joshua while they stood on the top of that rock on the day of his accident (or, was it really an accident?).

"How did he know?" asked Josiah aloud, of no one in particular.

"How did he know what?" asked Zachary.

"Oh, nothing. Just thinking out loud again," Josiah replied, smiling.

Quickly they finished their jerky, eager to cross the river. Mustgofast seemed to sense his master's zeal as he hurried him along.

Down by the river everyone sat to remove their shoes and socks and to roll up their pant legs. Everyone wore dungarees as they traveled.

"Hey, Josiah," whispered Mr. Jack. "Why don't you keep your shoes on, get up on that horse of yours, and cross the river that way? You know? That way you won't get wet." He smiled at his young friend.

"Did you hear that?" asked Josiah of Mustgofast. "Come over this way," he whispered. The horse obeyed as Josiah stood on a rock and bolted onto the back of Mustgofast. In a flash they were on their way. Mustgofast started off so quickly that if it had not been for the string attached to Josiah's hat, it would have been thrown to the ground.

These are the moments that dreams are made of. The little mustang never slowed at the approach of water, but seemed as excited as Josiah that finally they were together again, even as it should be. The river was wide, but not too deep. When they hit the bank on the other side, Mustgofast was in a full gallop. Josiah had no idea where the horse would take him, but he wasn't worried. He felt more than safe on the back of the one who had been so sensitive as to help save the life of his friend.

Across the meadow and up the hill toward the ranch ran the horse with his boy. Neither could have been any happier than at this moment. The wilderness was left behind them; they had reached the Promised Land, and it felt good.

Finally, Josiah reigned in Mustgofast, though he still sat upon his back. Down the hill he watched as Joshua, that is, Randy, led the one hundred, forty-four into the Promised Land. Mr. Jack walked with Patty in the back. Pete and Joshua drove the wagon up the hill.

Now this was something worthy of some film footage, thought Josiah. It was a sight to behold. It didn't matter though, that Zach wasn't here with his camera, for Josiah would never forget it.

He leaned forward and stroked the neck of Mustgofast. "Isn't this neat, Mustgo?" he asked, his heart full of something he couldn't quite identify that he would have had a hard time putting into words. The horse whinnied as he answered his boy, that indeed it was.

EPILOGUE

That day they set up their tents in the meadow not far from Randy's ranch house or from the clear river that ran through the meadow. There were simply too many of them to sleep in the house that had been built for the ranch hands some years ago before Sylvie had died. Mr. Jack and Mrs. Patty had been invited to stay in the main house, and, of course, the leaders had to stay with their tribes. Pete and Josh offered to take over the leadership of the Levites since Randy's injuries.

After doing their laundry and eating lunch, Randy came down and told the leaders that they could assist their tribes if they wished in enjoying a horseback ride in the enclosed pen outside of the barn. Some of the tamer horses would be brought in so as not to offer trouble for those who were not riders.

One of the few ranch hands that remained was told to go assist Juanito with a particular horse and to go riding on one of the trails with Josiah and his mustang, Mustgofast if they wanted to.

Of course all the boys wanted to go, but there were not enough knowledgeable adults to attend to them so for now it was out of the question; it would be only Josiah and Juanito. Though those who had come with Josiah would certainly have loved to go with them, everyone understood and even agreed that this was as it should be, given the circumstances. All of them were happy for the two and envy was not even part of the formula. Clearly, they were heroes, and how wrong the group would have been not to acknowledge it, since they all recognized it. Anyway, they were all having a wonderful time.

Looking very much like seasoned cowboys with their boots, dungarees, and western hats, the boys left after lunch to go trail-riding. Neither of them could contain their excitement. Even the man who was taking them out seemed excited.

As he was explaining one thing and another about the ranch, he shared with them that it had been a long time, actually since before Sylvie died, that he had taken anyone out riding.

"The horses these days, he said, "don't get much exercise. I think that even they are happy to get out and feel like they're earning their keep. I know I am! And, I understand," he continued, smiling, "that it is my privilege to be escorting two heroes."

Josiah smiled and Juanito smiled with him, though he didn't understand the comment. That's OK, though, because, of course, when they returned, Josiah planned to explain it all to the translator.

"By the way," the man said, "my name is Pedro. I was born in Sonora, Mexico, just south of the border. Does your friend understand English?" he asked of Josiah.

"No, he doesn't," smiled Josiah.

"No problem," said Pedro and he began to repeat what he had just spoken to Josiah in Spanish.

"You don't even look Mexican," said Josiah innocently.

"Why," responded Pedro, "what is a Mexican supposed to look like? Actually, my mother was as blond as you are. She was the daughter of an American missionary. When she first gave her life to the LORD she was just a child. My grandparents moved back to Colorado when she was a teenager and then lost touch with the Mexican church until they returned for a visit some years later. 'The rest,' as they say, 'is history'.

We've been part of the ranch for years. My wife Bea cooks for us guys here on the ranch. There aren't many of us left but there are enough that we get together and pray all the time for our boss, Randy. I think the LORD has done something very special for him during his time with you. He said he would share it with us tonight."

Josiah was overwhelmed by the loyalty of this friend. He hoped that when he grew he would have a friend like this. Who knew, maybe he and Juanito would have a friendship like that. It reminded him of the story of David and Jonathan. Meme' would say that usually you can count those types of friendships on one hand or less in a whole lifetime. That seemed about right to Josiah, for, even though he didn't have many years behind him, he imagined that it was true.

As they rode the trail, Mr. Jack, Patty, and Randy sat in the living room of Randy's home. It was rustic, well-kept, and smelled like home should smell. The tones of the wood on the walls, floor, and ceiling, were strong and the grains in each board added to the whole picture.

They sat in heavy wooden rockers that had been hand-fashioned and made by Randy himself. Heavy cushions made the chairs look inviting and comfortable enough to fall asleep in. Jack and Patty could not remember ever feeling more at home than at this moment.

They had just finished discussing how that until the boys left, they would be provided for in this land of milk and honey. There would be no more beans, beef jerky, or flatbread.

Beginning the following morning people would be here from the church; friends of Randy's, who would cook meals suitable for heroes, in honor of what the LORD had done in the life of Randy. These were willing even before they even knew the story.

"I want to show you something," said Randy, breaking the comfortable silence.

He withdrew an envelope from the table beside him.

"I had this drawn up before I went on this trip; even before I met you, on what I felt was the direction of God."

With that he handed Mr. Jack the envelope. "Go ahead," he said, "read it."

Mr. Jack opened it to see an official document.

"In short," Randy began, "it is a paper turning over the remainder of Sylvie's life insurance policy which has been kept in an estate account since her death. Isn't it funny, that I could never even use those words before? Now, I have no problem with them," he said, examining his hands and smiling. "It's OK now."

"Anyway," he continued, "I used what was necessary to bury her and haven't touched it since. We had insurance that more than covered her hospital expenses. There is a small family plot up on the side of the hill, overlooking the valley below and the river. It was Sylvie's favorite spot on the ranch. She and Richie have stones side-by-side up there. She loved a white picket fence and so they have that too. Isn't that nonsense, Jack? There is nothing in the view, the stones, or the fence that they need now. Of course, without thinking it through, I did that for my peace of mind, not for them."

"And, is anything wrong with that?" asked Jack of his friend. "I don't think so. For a time, while the LORD dealt with you, you were comforted by it."

"I guess you're right," he replied. "Anyway, I talked with my lawyer when I heard about this trip and asked him to see about turning the balance of this account, which is quite substantial, to benefit your work with the Kurds. I'm sure it will help, and I know that God is behind it."

Jack looked at the paper and was overwhelmed by the gift of generosity. Even Jack could not clearly visualize how much this would help and how far it would go. "God bless you, Randy," he said, clearly moved beyond any more words.

"Thank you, Jack. He has, and more than you can imagine. I'm glad the boys came along on this trip, but clearly this whole tour of Stopping Places was for me. The LORD must love me so much to go to all this trouble and involve so many players. I hope you will remember me when that little man, Josiah, comes up with his next big idea."

"And, I hope he'll remember me," said Mr. Jack honestly, "and that he never outgrows his need to be simply Josiah. Listen carefully, Randy," he said.

Out across the meadow as they entered the area closer to the barn everyone could hear Josiah loudly and clearly, "Yee haw, Mustgofast! Go, Boy!" It was as though they flew across the meadow, the horse and his boy. They had an understanding and a bond which few enjoy.

"Could there ever have been another horse like Mustgofast?" wondered Josiah.

And, if I didn't know any better, it seemed that Mustgofast was thinking too, "Was there ever a boy like Josiah?"

CHARACTERS

Though this is a work of fiction most of the
characters are real.
There is no ***Stopping Places*** mission or a ***Mustgofast***.
The ranch and the ranch hands are fictitious.
Josiah and his family are real
as is his church and their burden.
Jack Harris, his wife Patty,
and their sons Pete and Joshua are real,
and so is the mission work amongst the
Kurds in Northern Iraq.
The struggle of a long-forgotten people there is by
no means a fable, nor is the trail of blood and devastation
that Saddam Hussein has left behind.
A good work has been started;
homes are being built;
medical teams have been brought in;
and the gospel is being preached
and received in the hearts of these hungry people.
A new hope has arisen amongst those who seemed,
even to themselves, previously without hope.
It is not a big work, but it is a start,
and it is good not to despise the day of small beginnings,
after all;
Look how ***small*** is the ***tiny mustard seed...***

He hath sent me to bind up the brokenhearted,
To proclaim liberty to the captives,
and the opening of the prison
to them that are bound…
Isaiah 61:1

If you would like to forward any tax-deductible offering to help support the mission of Jack Harris
Please send to:

Mission Global Harvest (Iraq)
P.O. Box 1769
Rancho Cucamonga, CA 91730

One fourth of all proceeds from this book will be sent to:
Global Harvest ~ Iraq

Dr. Valerie A. Beauchene has written and published several works.

The following is a list of some of them:

A Teaching Series
The Wonders of Practical Christianity…

As Lively Stones
Solid Foundation

I Have Found the Book
The Power of a Tender Heart

Run For Your Life
The Icy Grip of Fear

Called by Name
In the Shadow of the Almighty

The Paralysis of Unforgiveness
Sexual Abuse and Other Critical Violations

To Whom Has the Arm of the Lord Been Revealed
The Fourfold Work of the Cross

Of Sinking Ships and Broken Walls
The Repairer of the Breach

Skeletons in the Closet
Curses and Dirty Genes

Rest for the Weary
All Ye That Labor

A Mind to Work
Offense, Defense, and Fencing

Hope for Laodicea
I Have Asked God

Touch Not the Unclean Thing
Because of Love

Still More for the Serious Scholar:

Shekinah Glory
Living Waters From the Rock That is Higher Than I

Rise and Shine
A Trilogy on Revival For the Christian

Red Camo
Ultimate Survival – A Post Rapture Handbook

~~~~
~~~~

And Now For Young Adults:

Every Kid Should Be Someone's Hero Series

The Teacher

Entertaining Angels

The Making of a Twenty-First Century Hero

Who Cares About a Stinkin' Ol Rabbit Anyway?

The Story of Mustgofast

The Auction

Angels Two

Stopping Places

Also Biblical Fiction for Young Adults:

If I Had Been There Series

Call Me Esther

Suffer the Little Children

Let My Son Go

The Little People

The Flute

Son of my Sorrow

And Now:

Little Heroes Series

The Middle Child

The Small but Mighty Mouse

If Wishes Were Wool

ABOUT THE AUTHOR

Dr. Valerie Beauchene and her husband
Rene serve as senior pastors of
TABERNACLES OF GRACE CHAPEL
in Danielson, Connecticut.
She has a Doctorate in Theology,
and a Master's degree in Biblical Studies
from Colorado Theological Seminary
in Denver, Colorado. She is also a member of the
American Association of Christian Counselors.
Val has traveled extensively, preaching and teaching
throughout the United States and internationally.
She and her husband have raised six children:
Richard, Rose, Lee, Robert, William, and Joshua.
They are blessed with sixteen grandchildren:
Cameron, Christopher, Zachary, Josiah,
Abigail, Tabitha, Jeremiah, Eben,
Anneliese, Samantha, Vanessa,
William, Tyler, Asaph,
Genevieve, and Jakob.

For ministry contact:
valeriebeauchene@yahoo.com

Check out her website:
www.counselinginchrist.com